Heir

KATEE
ROBERT

*To everyone who was Team Damon, Team
Spike, and far too into Dimitri Belikov.*

Heir is a dark and incredibly spicy book that contains dubious consent, blood play, patricide, pregnancy, blood, gore, murder, explicit sex, vomiting (caused by pregnancy), discussions about abortion, abusive parent (father, historical, off-page), attempted sexual assault (alluded to, nongraphic), and attempted drugging.

Copyright © 2022 by Katee Robert
Cover and internal design © 2022 by Sourcebooks
Cover design by Katee Robert
Cover photo by Ironika/Shutterstock
Internal design by Laura Boren/Sourcebooks
The publisher acknowledges the copyright holder of the individual work as follows:
Heir © 2021 by Trinkets and Tales LLC

Sourcebooks and the colophon are registered trademarks of Sourcebooks.

All rights reserved. No part of this book may be reproduced in any form or by any electronic or mechanical means including information storage and retrieval systems—except in the case of brief quotations embodied in critical articles or reviews—without permission in writing from its publisher, Sourcebooks.

The characters and events portrayed in this book are fictitious or are used fictitiously. Any similarity to real persons, living or dead, is purely coincidental and not intended by the author.

All brand names and product names used in this book are trademarks, registered trademarks, or trade names of their respective holders. Sourcebooks is not associated with any product or vendor in this book.

Published by Sourcebooks Casablanca, an imprint of Sourcebooks
P.O. Box 4410, Naperville, Illinois 60567-4410
(630) 961-3900
sourcebooks.com

Also published as part of *Court of the Vampire Queen* in 2022 in the United States of America by Sourcebooks Casablanca, an imprint of Sourcebooks.

Cataloging-in-Publication Data is on file with the Library of Congress.

Printed and bound in the United States of America.
POD

1

I CAN FEEL MALACHI'S HEARTBEAT. IT THROBS IN MY chest, a steady thump that would be reassuring if it wasn't so foreign. After all, it's not as if I'm lounging with my head on his chest the way I have many times in the last month. Malachi isn't even in the house.

He's across the county, the miles stretching between us.

I rub the back of my hand against my sternum, but if the last four weeks have taught me anything, it's that the sensation of multiple hearts nestled up against mine is magical in nature rather than physical. Malachi assures me that I'll get used to it eventually, which might actually be reassuring if his dark eyes weren't worried every time he looks at me. Better than Rylan, who won't look at me at all. I still don't understand why he hasn't left our little nest and taken his chances on his own. I don't understand him.

And Wolf?

Wolf, true to form, offered to carve open my chest to relieve me of the sensation.

"Stop it."

I don't look over as Rylan's icy words cut through the stillness of the loft. "You're talking to me now? How novel." I drop my hand and then have to curl it into a fist to resist going back to rubbing my sternum when Malachi's heartbeat kicks up a notch. The feeling in my chest intensifies, signaling proximity. "He's coming."

"About time," Rylan mutters.

At that, I finally face him. "It's been a month. Leave if you hate it with me that much."

"I would if I could." He practically hurls the words at me. His hand goes to his chest, mirroring me. He looks just as perfectly put together as he has from the moment I met him, his dark hair cut short on the silvered temples, his endless supply of suits without a wrinkle out of place. The only time I've seen him remotely rumpled was the night we all fucked, subsequently awakening my powers and landing us in this mess.

Together.

Whether we like it or not.

"Just kill me then. It's what you wanted from the beginning."

His eyes flash silver, the only sign that I've gotten beneath his skin. I shouldn't be so petty as to enjoy aggravating Rylan, but he's like a wall of knives I brush against with every movement. Malachi and Wolf might not be overly comfortable being tied to me, but at least they *like* me a little. Rylan's hated me from the start—a very mutual sentiment—and now we can't escape each other.

"Would that I could." He turns and stalks to the balcony doors, pausing to strip and systematically fold his clothing over the chair set there for what I assume is entirely that purpose.

I know what's coming, and as such, I should look away. But I've had so few pleasures in my life that I find myself unable to resist a single one, no matter the source. A naked Rylan is a pleasure, what comes next even more so.

He's gorgeous in an entirely different way from Malachi and Wolf. His suits do a good job of masking his strength, but out of them, he looks nearly as big as Malachi. He also has little dimples at the top of his ass that, despite myself, I want to lick. As much as I'd like to blame the bond for that, the truth is that I found this asshole attractive even before the night the bond snapped into place.

He steps out the doors and there's—I'm not sure how to explain it—a ripple, almost. As if reality gives a little shudder, a tiny tear, and then Rylan is gone and a giant black bird perches on the balcony in his place. A flap of its massive wings and he's gone, flinging himself out into the darkness.

He's moving quickly in the opposite direction Malachi is coming from, putting miles between us with ease. I feel each one like a nail driven into my chest. I hate it. I *want* him gone, but the more distance he puts between us, the greater the urge to demand he return.

To force him to return.

I stomp down on the urge and turn away from the balcony. I don't care what Rylan says about seraphim. I don't care that I can no longer deny that I'm one of them. I don't care about their history of bonding with and abusing vampires. Doing that intentionally would make me no worse than my monster of a father, and *that* is something I'll never do.

Death is preferable.

I can feel Wolf downstairs, likely painting again. The man holds multitudes and while I can appreciate the beauty behind his art, it's highly disturbing. Wolf is chaos personified, and that truth is even more apparent when he paints. He might kiss me or try to cut my throat on our next meeting. I never know. He scares me, but a small, secret part of me likes it. I feel particularly *alive* when I'm dancing on the blade edge with Wolf.

I don't want that right now. I'm too tired, too frustrated. Wolf, predator that he is, will pick up on it immediately, and he won't be able to resist testing me. Testing the bond. It exhausts me just thinking about going a round with him right now.

We might have spent the last month together, but I should know better than to lean on these vampires. Even Malachi, for all his declarations of intent, hasn't known me nearly long enough to actually mean anything he says. More, considering the possibility of a future together is a far cry from agreeing to a bond that only death will sever.

I am surrounded by men, but I'm just as alone as I was in my father's compound. Separate. Other. Alternatively a threat and prey, depending on who's around. The only thing I ever wanted was freedom, and it's the one thing I'll never have.

Gods, I'm a little ray of sunshine tonight.

I move through the upper floors of the house that is our most recent lodgings. Despite Malachi's intentions of losing ourselves in the city, the plan fell through almost immediately. It took my father's people less than twelve hours to find us the first time. Since then, we've had to get increasingly creative, avoiding any properties directly linked to Wolf or Rylan and moving regularly. It still isn't enough to grant us true peace, but at least we're staying ahead of my father's hounds.

Barely.

The air shifts behind me, but I don't need to look to know who it is. Malachi. When we first met, he had a habit of surprising me by appearing unexpectedly without a sound. Now that we're bonded, he'll never be able to sneak up on me again. None of them will. That knowledge should reassure me, should offer some kind of layer of safety, but it's simply a reminder of how much has changed in such a short time.

"Do you think he knew?"

Malachi doesn't ask who I'm referencing. "I doubt it. Even if she was like you and tasted different than humans do, there are a lot of monsters in our world. Knowing your father, he wouldn't have risked bedding her if he suspected she had even a hint of seraph blood."

She. My mother. The source of my seraph powers that awoke a month ago in a bed filled to the brim with sex and blood, the chain that now binds me to these three bloodline vampires.

Not every vampire in our world is graced with magic. Those turned might get the near-immortal life spans, but that's the best of it. Even those naturally born barely have a leg up over the turned vampires.

No, the true power lies with the seven bloodline families, each with a specialization they pass from parents to children. There are other perks, including pleasurable bites, but the real focus is the magic. My father can get anyone to do anything he wants as long as they're in the same room and he's able to speak. He can also use his glamour to shift his appearance.

And now I have three bloodline vampires linked to me. Malachi with his fire. Wolf with his blood magic. Rylan with his shape-shifting. Practically an army of three, all vested in keeping me alive, because if I die, there's a decent chance I'll drag them all to hell with me. Aside from my father, little can touch me now. If I were a different person, maybe I'd be elated.

I never wanted any of it.

Malachi closes the distance between us and wraps his arms around me, tugging me back against his large body. If not for the way he sometimes looks at me, I might allow myself to sink into these little intimate moments. To believe that the future holds even a sliver of happiness for me.

"You're thinking too hard." Malachi rests his chin on the top of my head. "You and Rylan have been sniping at each other again, haven't you?"

"I didn't want this," I whisper. I can feel Rylan winging his way farther and farther from the house—from me. Eventually, he'll reach the limits of our bond just like he has countless times in the last month, and it will snap at him until he turns back. "Why can't he understand I hate this even more than you all do?"

"He's got a long and complicated history with the seraphim. When your memory is as long as Rylan's, it's difficult to get past old beliefs. Old fears." Malachi delves his hands beneath my shirt to bracket my waist. I try to resent that the feel of his hands on my skin instantly unwinds some of my tension. I try...and I fail. I want to blame *this* on the bond, too, but my attraction to Malachi has been there from the moment we met and only seems to grow stronger with time.

With a sigh, I lean back more firmly against him, letting him coast his hands up my sides. "I didn't want this."

"I know." He shifts to press a kiss to my temple, my cheekbone, my jaw. "Mina."

"Yes." An answer and permission, all rolled into one. Rylan may be staying as far from me as he can manage. Wolf is as changeable as the wind, wild for me and avoiding me by turns. Only Malachi is consistent in this.

I wish I could believe that it's simply because he wants me.

If I were anyone else, maybe I could. But I'm not. I'm the daughter of Cornelius Lancaster, the last bloodline vampire of his line. Up until a month ago, I was a freak, a powerless dhampir. Half human, half vampire, somehow missing the power that should come along with that mixing of vampire with human. Useless except as a pawn in my father's schemes, as a womb to fill with another bloodline.

I have power now, but that doesn't make me safe.

If my father discovers that I have not one but *three* bloodline vampires linked to me, he'll use me as a tool to bring them to their knees. I might not want to take their freedom and willpower, but he'll be only too happy to in order to boost his own power. Killing him might be possible, but it won't solve the problem, not when I have other half siblings who are ready and willing to step into his shoes.

We have one chance to avoid being hunted until the end of time.

I have to become my father's heir.

The only way to do *that* is to get pregnant before any of my half siblings do. Not exactly an easy feat when some of them have been trying since before I was born. Not to mention I don't even know how vampire and seraph and human mix together. Rylan claims it's possible—even probable—that I can conceive and quickly. I'm not so sure.

"Mina." Malachi's lips brush my throat. "It will work out."

"You don't know that."

"No more than you know that it *won't* work out." He kisses my neck. "Let me make you feel good for a little bit."

Let him make me feel good. Let him have another go at getting me pregnant.

I exhale slowly. At this rate, my racing thoughts aren't going to slow down without extreme measures. "Bite me."

Malachi, gods bless him, doesn't hesitate. He sinks his fangs into my skin. Just like that, every thought turns to mist in my head. I melt back against him. Every pull as he drinks from me has pleasure curling through my body. Yes, this. This is what I crave right now.

I reach back and fumble at his pants. I need him inside me and I need it now. "Please."

He withdraws long enough to pull my shirt over my head and skim off my pants. His clothing quickly follows, and he wastes no time carrying me to a nearby couch. It's as sturdy as all the other furniture in this house, as if it were built for giants instead of regular people. Malachi sets me down and goes to his knees in front of me.

In this position, he feels even larger than he is. Broad shoulders that taper down to a slim waist. Muscles strong enough to punch his way through concrete walls without breaking a sweat. Scars upon scars, his outsides matching my insides. I reach out and press my hand to the mangled flesh over his heart where someone tried to carve it out. He still hasn't told me that story. Maybe he never will.

I abandon that line of thinking and dig my hands into his hair. It's just as long and dark as mine, though he's got a bit more wave in it. "I need you."

"Not yet." He presses me back against the couch and kisses his way down my stomach, his beard scraping against skin already overly sensitized by his bite. "I'm ravenous for you, Mina."

This. This right here is why I can't quite believe Malachi is only in this because he has no choice. We might be trapped together, have been trapped since the moment we met: first in that old house by my father's blood ward and now by the bond that strums between us with every beat of our hearts. If it was only the bond, Malachi would fuck me and nothing else. I'd hardly complain if that was all we did.

Instead, he's bringing me pleasure in a multitude of other ways every chance he gets.

In particular, he loves eating my pussy as much as I enjoy his mouth on me.

His breath ghosts against my clit and I shiver. "Well, if you insist."

Movement behind him has me startling. I was so focused on Malachi, I didn't feel Wolf approaching. He stands outlined by the doorframe, his lean form clothed in his normal eccentric mix of dark pants, a graphic T-shirt with a band I've never heard of, and suspenders. He gives me a feral grin. "You started playing without me."

Malachi doesn't lift his head, each word vibrating against my heated flesh. "Get over here, then."

2

WOLF'S ALREADY MOVING. HE STRIPS SLOWLY, HIS GAZE sliding over Malachi's ass, his bare back, to me. He looks at us like he can't decide if he wants to eat us or fuck us. Apparently I'll be dancing on the bladed edge with Wolf tonight after all. "So many toys, so little time."

Malachi ignores him and then his mouth is on me properly, his tongue sliding between my folds. Kissing my pussy just as thoroughly as he kisses my mouth. A moan slips free and the last of my worry slips away. It will still be there when we're finished. I tighten my grip in his hair, lifting my hips to rub myself against his tongue. It feels good, but I know Malachi. It's about to feel even better.

As if he can hear my thoughts, he bites me, his fangs on either side of my mound. Pleasure surges through me, as if the first bite readied me for exactly this moment. I come so hard, I scream, bucking against him. He grabs my hips and pins me in place, each pull making my orgasm crest higher and higher until my very voice gives out.

Only then does he give me one last lick and lift his head.

Wolf is there in an instant, claiming Malachi's mouth. I lie there and watch them kiss, a savage meeting of predators that should scare me but only turns me on more. They're not mine, no matter what the bond and Rylan think. They're not mine...but in this moment, they almost feel like they could be.

Wolf tugs Malachi's head back and licks the blood and me off his lower lip. He shudders. "Exquisite."

"You first." Malachi stands and pushes Wolf down on the couch next to me. "Suck my cock while you're at it."

Wolf's grin is...well, *wolfish*. I'm reminded yet again that these men—including Rylan—have a history that precedes my birth by centuries. Friendship and more, even if they had some sort of falling-out that I still don't have the details on.

I don't have the details on a lot of things when it comes to these bloodline vampires.

There's no time for my worries to take hold, though. Not with Wolf hauling me to straddle him and wrapping a fist around his cock. He doesn't hesitate to guide his blunt head to my entrance. I'm ready, more than ready, but I still have to work myself down his length in small strokes to take his size. I brace my hands on his shoulders as I do, looking down into his pale eyes that are already edging crimson the way they do when he's feeling strong emotions... Or drawing on his power.

I feel an answering pull in my clit, my blood rising to his call as he guides it to further my pleasure. I gasp and sink the rest of the way onto him. "I love it when you do that."

"I know."

Malachi barely waits for Wolf to seat himself entirely within me before he leans over the couch and then Wolf's sucking him down. I rock my hips as I watch him fuck Wolf's mouth, so turned on I can barely think straight.

He won't finish like this. They never finish anywhere but inside me these days.

I push the thought away and focus on riding Wolf's cock as he uses his power to call blood to my clit and nipples. It makes me so sensitive, it almost hurts, but I drink up the near pain with the same fervor that I consume the pleasure. I need more. Endlessly more.

I look up to find Malachi watching me. He doesn't break his stride, his fingers digging into Wolf's pale blond mohawk as he keeps up that punishing rhythm that demands a submission I don't know the other man is capable of. In these moments, I'm reminded that no matter how soft Malachi can occasionally be with me, he's truly the one who holds our little foursome together.

Not me.

As if he can sense my mood shifting, he reaches down and hooks the back of my neck, towing me closer to Wolf. "Drink from him."

"But—"

"Do it, little dhampir." His voice is slightly ragged as he fucks Wolf's mouth, but his eyes are intense on me. "How are you going to get stronger if you shy away from this?"

How indeed?

The worst part is that I *liked* drinking from them before the bond snapped into place. Whiskey is great, but bloodline vampire blood is like bottled lightning. The problem is that we don't know what exchanging blood is doing to the bond. All I know is that I crave drinking from all three of them with an intensity I can't blame on the pleasure I get from their blood. "But..."

Wolf makes the decision for me. He pulls a knife from somewhere and slices a long line down the length of his neck. Blood gushes and I'm closing the distance to press my mouth to the wound before I have a chance to reconsider.

Fucking Wolf is amazing.

Fucking Wolf while drinking his blood is like going from 2D to 3D. Every nerve ending lights up, even ones I'm pretty sure don't actually exist in the physical world. His power surges into me even as he grabs my hips and fucks up into me. It's so good. Too good. I try to hold out, to make this last, but my control is less than nothing when it comes to these men. I orgasm hard, crying out against his skin, his blood on my tongue.

He follows me over the edge, his fingers pressing so hard into my skin that I know I'll have bruises...at least for a few minutes before my increased healing abilities take care of them.

It's only when I'm being lifted off Wolf's cock that I realize Malachi stopped fucking his mouth a few moments ago. And then *he's* inside me, wedging his cock into me. Malachi doesn't give me time to recover, to move, to do anything but take him. He braces one hand on my hip and one on the couch next to Wolf's shoulder, and then he fucks me against the other man's chest.

Wolf grabs my hair and uses his hold to maneuver my head to

the side, baring my neck. It's all the warning I get before he bites me. I orgasm instantly, already primed from everything we've been doing up to this point. The bastard doesn't stop, though. He keeps sucking, timing it with Malachi's thrusts, driving my orgasm higher and higher.

My body gives out before they do.

I collapse, held in place between them as they finish. Wolf licks my neck, a sizzling feeling there telling me that he used his own blood to heal the bite. Malachi grinds deep into me and curses, filling me up.

Maybe this will be the time I get pregnant.

I know that's the goal, but part of me can't help hoping that it takes a little longer. Selfish. So fucking selfish of me. I'll feel bad about the thought later. Right now, I don't have the energy to do more than lay against Wolf's chest and relearn how to breathe.

This should be enough.

I have two sexy as hell vampires who have just fucked me within an inch of my life. The echoes of that last orgasm are still settling in my bones. Wanting more, craving more, is so beyond selfish.

Wanting *Rylan* is the height of foolishness.

I close my eyes, and even without trying, I can feel him down the length of the bond. He's miles away now, winging a circle with the house at the center. I might loathe the man, but my magic—my body—craves him with an unholy strength.

I wish there was someone I could talk to about seraphim. I didn't even know they existed until a month ago, and the only one of the three vampires that seems to know anything is Rylan. Unfortunately, he isn't talking. Or, rather, if it involves anything but icy silence or cold comments, he's not interested. He hates the seraphim, which means any information he has will be tainted by that emotion. It might be justified—hard to argue that it isn't— but that doesn't mean it's helpful.

But if there's a seraph left alive, they're deep in hiding. I can't pin my hopes on finding that needle in a haystack, especially when I'm not even certain it exists. No, there's no easy solution for me. I'm going to have to muddle through as best I can.

Malachi eases out of me and drops down on the couch next to us. A faint sheen of sweat glistens on his skin, and even as exhausted as I am, I want to lick him. Gods, I can't get enough of either of them.

He looks at us and gives that slow smile of his. "You're both a mess."

"It's your fault." I leverage myself up enough to press my fingers to the blood coating my chest from where I was rubbing against Wolf. It's already going tacky. "Both your fault."

"Guilty." Wolf stretches beneath me, lifting us a few inches off the couch. "I'd say I meant to be more careful with the knife, but—"

"You'd be lying." Despite everything, I find myself smiling at him.

"Yep." He drags his pale gaze over me. "Besides, you look good in my blood. You should wear it more often."

I blink. I'd say he's joking, but the way he's looking at me isn't amused at all. We just fucked, and he's staring at my body like he wants to clean me up with his mouth. "Wolf?" I don't mean for his name to come out as a question, but it happens anyways.

"You can take more, can't you, love?"

"Wolf." The word is carefully neutral, Malachi watching us both closely. I can't decide if he's trying to encourage the other man or deter him.

Wolf grins, flashing fang. When we first met, I thought it was a lack of control that causes him to do that. Now I know that it's just pure Wolf. He wants to flash fang so he does. It's as simple as that. He cups my breasts, dragging his fingers through the blood coating my skin. "Don't play so restrained, Malachi. We both know you'd like nothing better than to spend a month straight with her on your cock, filling her up over and over again until you plant a babe in her womb." He lowers his voice, speaking as if intent on seduction. "It makes you crazy that I'm fucking her, doesn't it? That I might be the one to father the child that makes her heir."

"That's enough."

"Is it?" Wolf lightly pinches my nipples. "Malachi, so calm and collected and in control." He laughs. "What a liar you are. She might believe you, but I know the truth."

Tension winds around us, tighter and tighter and having nothing to do with sex. No, there's the threat of violence on the air. "That's enough," I say, echoing Malachi's words.

"Would you kill me to get her to yourself?" Wolf hasn't stopped touching me, but all his attention is on the other vampire. I might as well be a cup of tea he's using to keep his hands busy. "Would you betray our history for *her?*"

Malachi hasn't moved. It doesn't seem like he's even breathing. "Would you?"

Just like that, the tension bleeds out of Wolf and he grins. "Time will tell, won't it?"

My desire has gone up in smoke, leaving only ashes in its wake. Bond or not, I am a fucking person and they're talking over my head like I'm a toy they're not inclined to share. "Let me go." I grab Wolf's wrists and pry his hands off my breasts. He lets me, which is just as well. I'm not sure what I'd do if he kept touching me while I'm this angry. "I'm done."

"Mina—"

"No." I struggle to my feet and point at Malachi. "I don't want to talk to you, either. I'm going to take a shower and then I'm going to bed. Alone." I make it one step before my anger gets the best of me. "I don't know if you need to fight or fuck your way to the end of this conversation, but you obviously don't need me here for it. Good night."

Neither of them say a word as I stalk out of the room. Of course they don't. I'm not required for this pissing match. I'm not required for *anything* important.

Except, oh yeah, I'm the reason we were able to break the blood ward keeping Malachi trapped in that house for decades.

And my damned womb is going to be the thing that unseats my father and allows them to finally stop being hunted by him and his people.

None of that matters, though. Bond or not, I'm still not convinced they see me as more than a tool for their endgame. Even Malachi betrays that when he gets like this, snarling and snapping over me like I'm a piece of meat in his possession.

No one gives a shit what *I* want.

3

I STALK INTO THE ROOM THAT I'VE CLAIMED AS MY own. Most nights, Malachi shares it. Wolf's here more than half of the time, too. Not Rylan. Never Rylan. He alone doesn't seem to have a use for me, which should irritate me, but right now it's almost a relief.

Almost as if my thoughts summoned him, the curtains billow out from the window and then he's there, a dark silhouette against the full moon in the shadows of the room. The shadows clothe him well enough, but I know he's naked. He always is after shifting back to human.

I stop short, planting my feet against the nearly overwhelming need to go to him. To run my hands up his bare chest and rub as much of my skin against his as I can manage. To take him into my body and ride until we're both sweaty and sated.

It's the bond. I *know* it's the bond.

The feeling in my chest isn't a tug any longer. It's a riptide, and I'm losing ground. I stagger forward a step. "What are you doing here?"

"I...couldn't stay away." He sounds like he's speaking through gritted teeth. "I tried."

My body takes me another step closer to him. It's like something else resides within my skin, a force I can't fight; I don't even know how to try. I grab the footboard of the bed. "Leave. I don't..." The surge in my chest gets stronger. "I can't control this."

"I can't leave. It won't let me." He says the words with such finality. As if pronouncing a death sentence.

It's only then that I notice how his body shakes. He's fighting this as much as I am. My fingers release the footboard without my permission and I stumble another few steps closer. "I *hate* this."

Rylan catches my elbows, and even that touch is enough to dim the pressing magic a little.

I exhale shakily. "I'm sorry."

"Stop saying that." He tightens his grip. "Stop fucking apologizing to me."

I shouldn't find his anger reassuring. It shouldn't feel like a bridge forming between us, a shared experience that neither of us want. I can't help it. I rest my forehead against his chest and close my eyes. "I guess there are limits to this, too. Can't fly too far from me. Can't go too long without...this."

"Tell me to stop and I'll find a way."

I open my eyes and drag in a breath. "It will hurt both of us if you do."

"Still," he says through gritted teeth. "Wolf can cause injuries serious enough that regenerating will take up all my strength. It'll buy time."

I blink. "Would you rather we do that?" I'm not sure how I feel about the idea that he might prefer to be maimed than to have sex with me, but I'm not exactly frothing at the mouth to fuck him, either. Still...

Rylan's muscles clench beneath my palms. I don't even remember putting my hands on his chest. He curses. "No, I don't want that. I resent the hell out of this bond—out of *you*—but that doesn't change the fact that I want you. Fucking you is no hardship, Mina."

"No hardship." My laugh comes out jagged. "It is if we don't choose this."

"Tell me to stop and I'll find a way," he repeats.

That's the thing. I don't want him to stop. I can blame the bond, but the truth is that I've been drawn to Rylan since I first saw him. I've hated him, resented him, but neither of those feelings have been enough to combat the sheer desire that licks at me every time we get too close. "I won't ask that of you," I whisper. I'm not even sure which outcome I'm talking about.

Rylan doesn't ask.

He yanks me against him, plastering us together. He takes my mouth. It can barely be called a kiss. It feels like an attack I'm only too happy to meet halfway. This is what I need. If we must do this, we'll do it our way. Angry. Just shy of violent.

I shove him back, and he twists just enough that he hits the wall instead of the open window. The impact still shakes us both.

Not enough. It's not fucking *enough*. Every time I turn around, I'm being reminded of how little control I have, how very much I'm at the whims of powers far beyond me. These vampires. The bond. Even my father. All have power where I have none.

I just want to forget.

Rylan spins me around and I barely catch myself on the window ledge. He doesn't give me time to recover, kicking my legs wide, and then he's there, shoving his giant cock into me. He's almost too big to make it work, even after fucking Malachi and Wolf earlier. Not that he cares. Not that *I* care. I press back, taking him deeper. "More."

His hands land on my hips. Sharp pain makes me jump. I twist to find that the tips of his fingers have...changed. Into claws. "Rylan?"

"Sorry," he grits out. "Can't control it."

He hesitates, but I'm having none of it. "Don't stop."

Rylan takes me at my word. He pounds into me, each stroke relieving a layer of pressure on the bond. I didn't realize how intensely his absence weighed on me until we're as close as two people can be, his body invading mine. The relief has me nearly giddy, which only stokes my anger hotter. "Harder."

The sharp pain of his claws digs in and then he's doing just as I command. Fucking me just shy of violently. Taking his frustrations out on my willing body.

Because I am willing.

I didn't choose the bond, but I choose *this*.

Pleasure instead of violent pain.

I look out over the grounds around this house. Trees crowd

close to the house, giving the impression of us being cut off from the rest of the world. Overhead, the moon is the only witness for what we do in the dark. Pleasure builds in time with the pounding Rylan's giving me. It feels so good that I want it to go on forever.

He has other ideas.

He loops an arm around my waist and hauls me away from the window. To the bed. I get a glimpse of his bloody claws, and for reasons I'm not inclined to examine, the sight makes me clench around his cock. Rylan growls and then he pulls out of me, flipping me around and shoving me down to the mattress.

The only other time we had sex, he was distant for the whole experience. He practically orchestrated it, overseeing things to ensure my power awoke and I broke the blood ward. Even when he was fucking my mouth, he was restrained and in control. There's none of that control now.

He covers me with his body, wrapping his claws around my wrists. "I can't stop."

"Don't." I lift my hips, angling to take his cock again. He shoves into me, and we release twin shaky breaths. This isn't enough, though. I knew it wouldn't be upon the first stroke. I tilt my head to the side. "Bite me."

"Mina." On his lips, my name sounds like a benediction and a curse, all wrapped up into one. He bites me with the speed of a striking cobra. Too deep. I can tell that from the moment his teeth sink into my skin. They're larger than normal, sharper. A predator's teeth meant for ripping and tearing.

Fuck.

This is bad.

The sharp spike of fear is instantly swallowed by the pleasure of his bite. I orgasm hard, wrapping my legs around his waist in an attempt to get him closer, deeper. To make this wave last forever. He keeps fucking me in a borderline frenzy, his mouth latched onto my neck. My blood is flowing freely, too freely, but I can't quite bring myself to care. Not when he's so close.

His strokes lose their steady rhythm and he grinds into me as he comes. I hear shouts in the distance, but I don't really care about that, either.

At least I don't until Rylan lifts his head and snarls. The sound is beastly and far too deep to have come from his throat. In fact, he feels bigger all around right now, as if he's put mass onto his muscled frame while I wasn't paying attention.

He pumps into me almost leisurely, but his eyes—now fully silver—are on something outside the bed. I start to turn my head but stop when pain flares to life with a strength that makes me gasp.

That brings Rylan's gaze back to me. His eyes drop to my neck and he licks his lips. Blood covers the lower half of his face. It covers everything. Him. Me. The bed. Too much blood, even for me.

"Rylan!" That's Malachi's bellow. Close enough to rattle my bones.

Rylan gives himself a shake. He's moving strangely, as if not quite at home in his body. Slowly, so so slowly, he releases one of my wrists and uses a claw to cut his neck. His blood joins mine on his skin, but I can't quite make my body obey my command to lift my head and drink.

Something akin to true fear flashes over his face. "Fuck."

"Feed her, you idiot!" That's Wolf. He sounds almost... worried.

Rylan carefully slides his hand under my head, his claws tangling in my hair, and lifts me as he lowers himself down. My lips touch his neck and fire lashes my tongue. Another swallow and I'm able to latch onto him. Not as well as he could with his superior teeth, but enough that I can drink freely from him. Each mouthful of blood chases away the cobwebs that had sprouted in my head. I swear I can actually feel my body knitting itself back together, muscle and veins and skin.

Gods, he really fucked me up.

He's already hard inside me again, and he starts to withdraw, but I dig my heels into the small of his back. I manage to lift my head enough to say, "Just a little more."

It might be my imagination, but Rylan makes a sound that's filled with relief. "Consider it done." His grip on my head goes gentle and he moves against me, in me, leisurely as I drink from him.

This time, when my orgasm comes, it's softer and nearly sweet and Rylan follows me over the edge immediately. He eases out of me but doesn't move away entirely. I'm shaking. Or maybe he's shaking. I can't tell.

Malachi and Wolf descend on us. Malachi yanks Rylan off me, his big hand wrapped around the other vampire's throat and murder on his face. I struggle to sit up, but Wolf is there, climbing behind me and pulling me between his legs to rest against his chest. He has a knife in one hand and presses the blade to his forearm. "You need more."

"Malachi." My voice is hoarse. I'm not sure if it's from fucking or damage done by Rylan's bite, and I don't care. "Get your hands off him."

"He almost killed you."

"*Let him go.*" My words ring with a foreign power, making my tongue feel like it's sparking. It surges out from me in an arrow aimed right at Malachi.

He drops his hand as if burned. Rylan staggers back a step and slumps against the wall. He looks like shit. I *feel* like shit. Tomorrow, I'll be worried about how close we got to the point of no return. I'll torment myself with how to balance the bond so it doesn't happen again. I'll do a lot of things. Tomorrow. "Just leave."

"Little dhampir."

"*Leave.*"

Malachi hesitates, clearly fighting the command. I'll regret this tomorrow, too. I close my eyes so I don't have to see him stalk out of the room, and I almost manage to contain my flinch at the way the door slams behind him.

Wolf shifts behind me and I open my eyes. "I'm angry at you, too."

"Be angry later. You need this."

I ignore his uncharacteristic seriousness and focus on Rylan. "Sit down before you fall down."

"Is that an order?" It's a token of how out of it he is that his question is barely tinged with frost instead of its normal iciness.

I slump back against Wolf despite my best efforts. Damn it, he's right. I need more blood. I'm dizzy and everything feels like it's too far away. "You want to collapse because of pride? Suit yourself."

Wolf presses his forearm to my lips. "Drink."

I do, greedy pulls of his blood into me. I don't know if it's because Wolf's bloodline controls power over blood or if I'm just feeling better already, but I can actually sense it healing me. I take two more pulls and then push his arm away. "That's enough."

"It's not enough." Wolf's arms tense around me as if he's considering restraining me, but he finally lets them drop.

I fight my way to the edge of the bed and stand on shaking legs. Even with Rylan's and Wolf's blood coursing through me, I'm not going to be okay for a bit. But I'm alive and walking around, so that's more than enough.

I stagger to Rylan, stopping just out of reach. For the first time since it snapped into place, the bond is quiet. It won't last; I know that now. I'm still going to appreciate the reprieve.

For his part, Rylan looks just as shell-shocked as I feel. His body has gone back to normal. Vampire teeth. Human hands, not a claw in sight. I hesitate. "Are you okay?"

His smile holds no mirth. "I should be asking you that question." His gaze lingers on my neck. I don't know him well enough to read his expression, but it looks almost tormented. "This fucking bond. I don't lose control. Not like that."

"I'm fine." My gravelly tone threatens to make a liar out of me. I gingerly touch my fingertips to the newly healed skin of my neck. "By tomorrow, there won't be a mark."

"Mina—"

I let my hand drop. I don't want his apologies. I'm not certain that's what he's about to say, but I don't give him a chance. "Come on. We need to clean up." The bed is ruined. Blood soaks the entire mattress. Changing the sheets won't help. I glance at Wolf. "Do you mind airing out the spare bedroom? I think we have some sheets left over from the last shopping trip." They're always on the list since we go through them so often. Blood is a hell of a stain to try to get out, but the real problem is that they keep getting torn up when our bedroom games get rough.

His pale gaze flicks between me and Rylan. Finally, he climbs off the bed and gives a theatrical bow. "As the lady commands."

"It wasn't a—" He's gone before I can finish. I sigh. "It wasn't a command."

"Semantics." Rylan still doesn't sound like himself. The icy distance that I find strangely comforting is nowhere in evidence. He doesn't even argue as I nudge him in the direction of the bathroom.

I'm weaving on my feet, exhaustion pulling at my body, but it feels important to do this. The why matters less than following my instincts in this situation, so I turn on the water, wait for it to heat up, and then give Rylan another nudge.

Again, he doesn't argue. He simply steps into the shower. But he catches my hand and tows me in after him. Neither of us speak. He doesn't comment on the way I scrub the blood off his chest and neck. I don't make note of how his leaning on me suggests that he's nowhere near as okay as he said.

By the time we're done, I can barely keep my eyes open.

Strangely enough, I'm not remotely surprised to find Wolf and Malachi waiting for us. Wolf wraps a towel around me and sweeps me off my feet, carrying me out of the room with quick strides.

Not quickly enough to avoid hearing Malachi's low words to Rylan. "I told you so."

4

I WAKE TO THE SOUND OF VOICES. THE MEN ARE IN THE next room, talking softly. I roll onto my back and open my eyes, staring up into the darkness of the bedroom. It would be the easiest thing in the world to pull the covers over my head and ignore what happened last night. What it signifies. Even if we ran to the very ends of the earth opposite each other, the bond would eat away at us until...

Could it kill us?

I wouldn't have thought it possible, but that was before it physically propelled me across the room to Rylan. Before it made him forget himself enough to partially shift.

I could let the vampires deal with this current mess. They're all older and more powerful than I am. I'm a fool if I think I can stand on equal footing with them in the coming confrontation, bond or no. They will always be stronger, always be more powerful.

If I hide, I'll remain a pawn for the rest of my life, however long or short that ends up being. Dhampirs live longer than humans, but they aren't borderline immortal like full vampires. I have no idea what the seraph lifespan looks like.

The list of what I don't know only seems to grow longer with time instead of shorter.

I sit up and sigh. There's no help for it. The easy way isn't the right way, and I've fought too hard for anything resembling freedom to simply hand off all the decision-making process to others. They might be more powerful, but *I'm* the linchpin in this mess.

Another soundless sigh and I leave the warmth of the bed and pull on the nearest piece of clothing—one of Malachi's shirts. He's updated his wardrobe a bit since we left the house, but he still favors the shirts that look like they'd be perfectly at home on historical romance novel covers. I like them. A lot. I'm swimming in all the white fabric, his tobacco and clove scent nearly as comforting as when he wraps his arms around me.

I'm still angry about last night. It irritates me to no end that I want *him* to comfort me while I'm mad at him. I inhale again, letting the last of my reservations fall away. As tempting as it is to hide from reality, I know all too well the reality will burst through the door without an invitation. Better to deal with things head-on.

The men haven't stopped talking, but with their superior senses, they all know I'm awake and moving around. I pad barefoot out of the spare bedroom, down the hall, and into the sitting room where they've got a fire going.

Rylan is standing by the window, the light of the early morning putting his features in stark contrast. He looks as tired as I feel, his cheekbones a little too gaunt on his handsome face. Wolf lounges on one of the chairs. He's got his leg dangling over the arm like an indolent king waiting to be entertained. Malachi sits on the couch, his elbows braced on his thighs. All three look at me with varying degrees of wariness.

I stop short. "We need to talk about last night."

Malachi holds out a hand, motioning for me to join him on the couch. I almost go to him through sheer habit, actually take a step in his direction, before the memories of last night crash over me again. How he looked like he was going to murder Rylan. How I magically compelled him to leave the room against his will.

I don't know if it's sleep still clouding my mind or if the situation is just becoming too stressful and I'm in danger of shattering. Right now, I need to be calm and collected, an impossible task when every breath feels like I'm drowning, drawing in water instead of the air I desperately need.

I drop into the free chair. Disappointment flashes over Malachi's face, but it's gone so fast, I'm half sure it's a trick of the firelight. I draw my knees up and wrap my arms around my legs. "We're in over our heads. I can't control the bond, and it's putting you in danger."

Wolf snorts. "None of *us* were the one bleeding out last night."

Rylan flinches, a barely perceptible movement I only catch out of the corner of my eye. I ignore it. "That was my fault. Or, rather, the bond's fault. It never would have gotten so out of control if the bond didn't exist and hadn't messed with our control."

"It was Rylan's fault." Malachi's body might appear relaxed, but he looks like he wants to shred something with his bare hands. "He knew there was risk involved with resisting the proximity the bond demands. He played with your life."

"That's enough."

"He's right." The words sound dragged from Rylan. "I knew there was a risk."

I finally look at him. Even now, with the bond mostly sated, I feel the urge to cross the room and press my mouth to his skin. I clear my throat. "I knew the bond was being affected by avoiding each other, too."

"You couldn't know what it meant."

That's about enough of that. I level a look at each of them in turn. "I am not a child who needs others to make the decisions for me or take responsibility for my actions. Maybe I didn't know the parameters of the bond, but there hasn't been a living seraph in three out of four of our lifetimes. None of us have experienced a seraph bond before. As a result, there will be mistakes."

"He almost ripped out your throat." Malachi's staring at me like he wants to wrap me up and shove me into a cage. All in the name of safety, of course.

This isn't an argument I'm going to win. It's written across all their expressions. I didn't expect this seriousness from Wolf, but he's surprised me a lot lately. Or maybe his self-preservation is stronger than his wildness. No one knows for sure what happens if I die, but we're all convinced it's bad.

Better to change the subject and circle back when I have an argument that might actually make them hold still long enough to listen. "You were awfully tense when I came in here."

Suddenly, they all find other things in the room to look at, avoiding my gaze. Alarm bells blaze through my head. "Have they found us again?"

"No. You're safe."

"Don't lie to her, Malachi. She's not safe. None of us are." Rylan's staring out the window as if seconds from stripping and shape-shifting into some animal so he can run as far and fast from this conversation as possible.

If my father's people haven't found us and it's not about last night... What else could possibly go wrong now? I glance from one to the other, finally settling on Wolf. The other two can hold out indefinitely if they decide I need to be left in the dark. Wolf won't. "Tell me."

"I—"

"*Wolf.*"

Malachi's sharp warning is like waving a red flag in front of a bull. Wolf laughs and slouches farther into the chair. "Nothing much, love. Just ways it might be possible to break the seraph bond without killing all of us in the process."

The possibility leaves me breathless. I slump back into my chair, my legs suddenly boneless. "We can do that?"

"Probably not," Rylan says darkly, still staring out the window. "If it could be done, more people would know about it."

Wolf rolls his pale blue eyes. "As I was telling *you*, seraphim were all but legend to most people until this happened.

Just because you've never heard of a way doesn't mean it isn't possible."

Something almost like excitement flickers through me. "How do we do it?" If there's a way to remove the bond, then my chance at freedom isn't gone after all. "What do you know?"

"So eager to be free of us." Wolf laughs again, a high, mad sound that raises the small hairs on the back of my neck. He drops his foot to the floor and straightens. "I know a guy."

"You know a *demon*," Malachi cuts in. His expression is carefully closed down, offering nothing at all.

I blink. Wait for someone to laugh and let me in on the joke. No one does. They're all watching me with devastatingly serious expressions on their face.

Demons.

Demons exist.

I don't know why I'm surprised. Seraphim are, at least according to a number of human religions, the holier counterparts to demons. Considering what my people have done to other supernatural creatures, maybe demons are cuddly do-gooders. I clear my throat, striving to sound like my world hasn't shifted on its axis yet again. "Are demons trustworthy?"

Wolf gives another of those wild laughs. "They're *demons*, love. Demon deals have the reputation they do for a reason. They're an option of last resort, reserved for the desperate."

"Ah." I press my lips together. "Well, we're desperate. How do we get a hold of a demon?"

Rylan frowns as if deciding to be present in the conversation for the first time since I walked into the room. "You're serious."

"Of course I'm serious. I know you think I'm a monster who wants to put a leash on your cock, but I didn't choose this bond any more than you three did. If it's not in play, then I have a chance to actually be free."

"Mina." I hate how reserved Malachi sounds. He's studying me with those dark, dark eyes. "Even if your father doesn't know that you're part seraph, he will hunt you until he's dead or you are. He can't afford to let you escape."

Because if I can escape, supposedly powerless bastard dhampir that I am, then anyone can.

I know Malachi's right, and I hate it. I take a slow breath. "We'll cross that bridge when we get to it. The bond has to take priority."

Wolf is watching me, too. For once, the ever-present mocking amusement on his face is nowhere to be seen. "The cost is always high for demon deals."

I don't say that I'm willing to pay it. I can't, not without knowing what it is. "I'm not prepared to rule out any option until we've fully explored it."

Malachi looks like he wants to argue, but Wolf has already jumped to his feet. "I'll see what I can do."

"*Now?*"

"No time like the present." He strides out of the room without a backward look. Knowing what I do of the man, he might be intent on his destination...or he might get distracted and disappear for a few days, only to show back up having totally forgotten his intentions. Wolf is as wild as his namesake and ten times as unpredictable.

Rylan starts for the door. "This won't work."

"Rylan." Malachi doesn't move, but his gaze tracks the other man. "You need to stop resisting. Last night can't happen again."

"Mind your own business."

It seems like every single conversation we have these days circles back to this fucking bond. I want to rip it out with my bare hands. "It's fine." I continue when it seems like Malachi might argue. "Leave it, please."

"Look at you, already acting like the heir." Rylan's gone before his cold words fully penetrate.

I can't work up even a half-hearted glare in response. Not when he's right. Not when I'm strangely grateful the unnatural peace from last night is no longer in play. *This* Rylan, I understand. When he's cold, he makes sense. Even the feral, out-of-control version of him is safer than the shell-shocked man who shared a shower with me. It's hard enough to keep him at a distance with the bond pulling at me when we actively hate each other. If there's a softening at all...

To distract myself, I look at Malachi, who doesn't seem any happier than he did a few minutes ago. I want to storm out of the room to avoid *this* conversation, too. Unfortunately, that's not a permanent solution. "I'm sorry about last night." I rush on before he can say anything. "Not about what happened with Rylan, though I'm sorry it worried you. But I'm sorry about after."

"Mina, come here."

I almost don't. My reasons for choosing this chair instead of the couch remain, but it's just the two of us now and I miss the feel of his body against mine. I want to blame that on the bond, but I've been drawn to this vampire since before it snapped into place. "We need to talk about it."

"We will." He motions with his fingers again, beckoning me. "Come here. Please."

Please.

Have I ever heard Malachi utter that word? I don't think so. That, more than anything, gets me up and moving around the coffee table to take his hand. He tugs me down to straddle him, but there's nothing sexual in the move. It's as if he wants the comfort of touching me as much as I crave touching him.

"I didn't know I could do that," I whisper.

"I suspected it was possible."

I blink. "You didn't think to say something?"

"Suspecting something and knowing it for truth are two different things, little dhampir." His gaze coasts over my face as if memorizing my features. "I won't say I liked the feeling, but if you hadn't done something, I might have killed Rylan. I...wasn't thinking clearly."

"Malachi." A bitter little laugh slips free. "We are such a mess."

"It's no surprise there's a learning curve on this. There is on all magic."

"I wouldn't know." Up until a month ago, I thought I hadn't inherited any magic at all despite the fact that most dhampir children of bloodline vampires get some kind of magical skill. Based on my father's bloodline, I should be able to glamour people. Instead, I was thought a dud and sent to Malachi as a brood mare.

Apparently my seraph blood stifled or overpowered the vampire genetics. I'm still not sure which is the truth. I don't know if I'll *ever* be sure.

The whole thing makes my head hurt if I think about it too closely.

"Mina." Malachi waits for me to look at him to continue. "We'll figure it out. Together. I'm not prepared to hold missteps against you while you're exploring the parameters of your powers. Do you intend to compel me again?"

"No!" I swallow hard and temper my tone. "Absolutely not."

"That's all that matters. Consider yourself forgiven." He hesitates. "I'm...sorry...as well."

His hesitance makes me smile a little. We really are an unmitigated mess. I glance at the doorway that the other two left through. "I hope Wolf's able to find that demon he was talking about. It could be the solution we need."

Malachi goes tense beneath me. "Are you really that eager to be rid of me?"

5

EAGER TO BE RID OF HIM? IS HE JOKING? I CRAVE Malachi like a fever in my blood. Even now, I can't help running my hands down his chest, tracing the lines of his muscles beneath his white shirt, so similar to the one I'm wearing right now. "You should be happy there's a chance to negate the bond."

"You're so quick to forget what I said before we left my home."

I sit back and stare. I don't understand why he's angry about this. "Being forcibly bonded is not something anyone wants."

"Don't tell me what I want, little dhampir." He coasts his hands up my thighs, beneath the hem of the shirt, to settle on my hips, tugging me until I'm pressed tightly against him. "We will explore this option if you insist, but I won't allow you to bargain anything you can't afford to lose."

I sigh, the sound almost a whimper as he rocks me against his hardening cock. "The price will be high regardless. That's to be expected."

"All the same."

I should just let him sweep me away with sex like he has every other time my stress winds me too tightly. I frown. "You were never this good at reading me before."

Just like that, his expression shuts down. "You're easy enough to read, Mina."

His lack of tell is a tell all its own. I put my hands on his shoulders and stare down at him. "Malachi, you missed blatant cues when I first moved in with you. Not all of that was intentional, so don't lie to me and tell me it was." When he still doesn't say anything, I press. "I thought the only side effect of the bond was being able to feel proximity. And now apparently my being able to command you."

"The magic you used on me last night might not be linked to the bond. Your father's glamour isn't just changing people's visual perceptions. He can command them, too."

I know that, have experienced it, but somehow the fact that I might be using a *vampire* power never really occurred to me. Still... I shake my head, trying to focus. "Stop trying to distract me. We're talking about the bond."

He finally says, "Feeling proximity to each other is a side effect of the bond, yes."

Careful. So fucking careful. Which means he's hiding something and not even doing it well. "Enough of this." I start to rise, but he clamps his hands on my hips, holding me in place. I glare.

"I'm going to go ask Wolf if he can feel my emotions. *He* won't lie to me." If only because he'll enjoy the chaos the confirmation will bring about.

"Mina."

"Malachi." I match his censoring tone. "I am not a child, and if you hide things from me, I'm going to resent it. Tell me the truth."

His sigh is nearly imperceptible. "Yes, I can...sense things."

"Things being my emotions." The sheer intrusion of it has my chest getting tight. This bond is bad enough. Knowing where they are at all times is horrible. I never thought to ask if it goes both ways, but of course it does. They know where I am without fail. It's how they recognize exactly how far the bond stretches before things get painful.

"Things being your emotions," he confirms. "Not all of them. I get spikes of pleasure or anger or fear. It only seems to be the extreme versions of them."

"I can't feel yours," I say numbly.

He lifts one hand to cup my face, moving carefully as if he expects me to flinch away. "All of us learned to shield a long time ago. It's a necessary skill."

Somehow, this just makes me feel worse. "A necessary skill for vampires and dhampirs with power."

"You have power now." He strokes my cheekbone with his thumb. "I'll teach you, little dhampir."

I want that, but I'm not quite prepared to let go of my complicated feelings about him hiding this. It's enough to make me wonder what else he's keeping from me, supposedly for my own good. "Why didn't you say something as soon as you understood what was happening?" Realization rolls over me. "That's how you knew things had gotten out of control with Rylan last night." It hadn't even occurred to me to question it before now. Vampire senses are incredibly strong, so it's likely they knew we were having sex even without the bond, but now that I think about it, I don't believe either Wolf or Malachi would have come into the room without an invitation. Not when Rylan and I are balanced so carefully at odds right now.

They felt my flash of fear when he bit me and it brought them running.

"Yes." He shifts his hand to cup my neck. "I didn't tell you before because I knew you wouldn't like this new development, and you're already under enough pressure."

Once again the urge rises to simply...let him handle this. I'm outmatched and outgunned and I don't know anything about magic. It would be so easy to let Malachi take charge. I can't do it. I close my eyes. "Don't keep things from me again. I realize that I'm hardly an asset right now, but the choices you make affect me, too. I can't make the right calls if I don't know all the info."

I can't make the right calls. How laughable. I haven't made a single fucking call.

"There's nothing else."

I wish I believed him.

Not for the first time, I wish we were just two people who'd met under normal circumstances. I don't even know how that would work. I can't imagine running into Malachi in a coffee shop or on a street or in the thousands of other places meet-cutes happen in fiction. Going on a normal human date? It defies comprehension. What a mess. I slump down against his chest, and he tenses a little like I've surprised him. I close my eyes. "I hate this."

"We're in an adjustment period."

That almost makes me laugh. Almost. "I am magically bound to three vampires who I barely know, two of whom would be only too happy to murder me."

"Wolf likes you."

I open my eyes and lift my head so I can shoot him the look that statement deserves. "Wolf might like me just fine. Sometimes. We both know that doesn't change the truth of my statement."

He shrugs a single shoulder. "None of us are going to hurt you. Last night was an anomaly."

Hurt is such a strange concept. I was a child when I realized that physical hurt is far preferable to the pain someone can cause with their words, with their willingness to lock me away and deprive me of their attention. Compared to that, being beaten is almost a relief. At least I know *that* pain will fade.

The pain and fear I felt last night were massively overshadowed by pleasure. Not to mention the easing of the pressure on the bond between me and Rylan. The cost is more than worth the reward from where I'm sitting, but I don't need to ask Malachi to know he doesn't agree.

"Teach me to shield."

"Tomorrow." He digs his hands into my hair and gives it a light tug. "After we spar."

A groan slips free before I have a chance to stop it. "I *hate* sparring." Even with Malachi's blood having nearly healed my formerly shattered knee, it's readily apparent that I'll never be as fast or strong as he is. Whatever else is true about the seraphim, they're nowhere near as physically superior as vampires are. Against a human? I can hold my own and then some. Against Malachi? I doubt I'll ever be able to. "You always kick my ass."

"You're getting stronger." The way he says it, I'm tempted to believe it's true.

I frown. "I'll never be a match for you."

"Of course not." He gives me a slow grin that has my stomach doing flips. "I'm older and stronger than you." He leans forward until his lips brush the shell of my ear. "You need to learn to fight dirty."

"I *do* fight dirty." I have since I realized I'd never win in a fair fight, a lesson I learned long before I ever met Malachi.

His chuckle is more like a rumble. "You're terrible at it."

"Wow, thanks. That's such an enlightening criticism."

"We'll invite Wolf to spar. He can teach you a thing or two."

I sigh. "I bet. Though it's going to end with me bitten and us fucking."

"Is that so bad?" Malachi shifts against me, pulling me back so our hips are sealed together. He's still hard, but he *always* seems to be hard when we get close. It's a little mind-blowing, but I'm not exactly complaining. I like fucking him. I like *him*. If this situation were different...

But it's not.

He might have enjoyed the sex before we were forcibly bonded when my powers emerged, but if last night proved anything, it's that now he doesn't have a choice. Neither of us do. "It is when the alternative is potentially death."

"Mina, I've wanted you since the moment I saw you." He guides me to roll my hips again, sliding one hand up my spine until my breasts press against his chest and I put my arms around his neck. His lips brush my ear. "Even in a frenzy and half-starved, I had to get my mouth on your pussy. You can't blame the bond for that."

No, but I could blame the whole being-half-starved thing.

I see his point, though. I don't know if I'm willing to accept it, but I see it. I draw in a harsh breath. "We're going to talk to the demon. Getting rid of the bond doesn't mean getting rid of you."

"It better not." His voice lowers, becoming nearly a growl. "Wolf wasn't lying yesterday. I have to make myself walk away from you, little dhampir. All I want is to chain you to a bed and fuck you until you're filled up with me. Until you're pregnant with *my* child."

Oh gods.

I shiver against him. "That, um, is the end goal."

"I don't give a fuck about the goal." He drags his mouth down the side of my neck, directly over where Rylan bit me last night. "I wanted that even before we decided usurping your father was the best option."

I shiver harder. "Oh." It would be so easy to believe him...

Why am I fighting this?

It doesn't matter what might have been because we can only deal with what *is*. And the reality of the situation is that Malachi and I—and Rylan and Wolf—are bonded because of my seraph blood. The reality is also that my father will hunt me—and Malachi, most likely—to the ends of the earth because we escaped his trap. The best way out of a future spent on the run is getting me pregnant so I can take the place as his heir. And then killing him.

Spending time wishing for things to be different from how they are is wasteful.

I tilt my head to the side, encouraging him. "I suppose we shouldn't waste any time."

"Mmm." He nips my neck, nowhere near hard enough to draw blood, and rocks me against his length again. "Take my cock out."

"So bossy," I murmur. I shift back just enough that I can reach between us to do as he commands. He fills my palm and then some, his size massive and familiar. I stroke him. "Hurry."

Malachi ignores me. He grabs a fistful of his shirt that I'm wearing and winds it at the base of my spine, lifting the hem until I'm bared from the waist down. The growl he makes has me whimpering. "So fucking perfect." It almost sounds like he's speaking to himself rather than to me. He palms my pussy, pushing two blunt fingers into me. He's fingered me more times than I can count in the last month, but it feels particularly possessive in this moment. As if he's reclaiming something he thought he might lose.

Something he *refuses* to lose.

"Did it feel good fucking Rylan, little dhampir?"

"Yes," I gasp. I try to rock my hips to take his fingers deeper, but his hold on the shirt keeps me hovering above him.

He idly fucks me, watching his large fingers slide in and out of my pussy. "He partially changed."

It's not a question, but I still feel compelled to answer. "Yes." I clutch at Malachi's shoulders. My thighs are shaking and he's just getting started.

His eyes go a pure, true black and he licks his lips. "Did his cock get bigger inside you?" He wedges a third finger into me. "Did he stretch you until it almost hurt?"

I claw at his shoulders, but I'm not going anywhere until he allows me to. "Yes," I sob out. "It felt amazing."

"I know." He says it so softly, I *know* he's not speaking to me. Just like I know that he and Rylan haven't rekindled some semblance of their former relationship the same way he and Wolf have. *They* might fuck each other nearly as often as they fuck me, but Rylan holds himself apart.

It strikes me that the flicker of jealousy in Malachi's dark eyes isn't directly solely at Rylan for fucking me. It's also at *me* for fucking Rylan.

I release his shoulders and place my hands on my hips. "He grabbed me here. His claws sank into me." There are still little divots in my skin, a reminder that all the blood I consumed went to keeping me alive instead of healing the smaller wounds completely.

"He held you in place while he fucked you." Malachi presses his fingers deeper and then twists his wrist, feeling for my G-spot.

"Yes." This time, when I rock my hips, he lets me ride his fingers. My voice goes a little rough. "He threw me on the bed and held me down."

Malachi exhales slowly. "You liked it."

"I loved it." The truth. I don't know why I love the rough fucking, the near-violent consumption of lust. In the end, knowing why doesn't matter. I love it, and that's good enough reason to do it.

He pulls his fingers out of me, but I don't have a chance to protest because he twists, taking us to the couch with him on top of me. Malachi doesn't give me time to adjust. He spreads my thighs wide and starts working his cock into me. Heat dances on my skin, but no flames appear. He hasn't lost control of his bloodline power since we left his house. I'm grateful for that fact; I love knowing I affect him deeply, but I don't relish the thought of having to flee yet another room because Malachi burned the hell out of it in the middle of sex.

"I like seeing his marks on you, little dhampir." His gaze lands on my throat again. I haven't looked in the mirror since I woke up, but if the pinpricks on my hips from Rylan's claws are still there, then no doubt I still bear a mark from his teeth. Malachi shoves all the way into me and braces himself on his elbows on either side of my body. He's pinning me in place but saving me from the majority of his weight.

He runs his nose over my throat. "I love smelling him on your skin." His tongue darts out to taste me. "This is how it should be. All three of us."

Pleasure courses through me, but my mind trips over what he just said. "You can *smell* him on me?" I shift, but Malachi isn't letting me move. "I took a shower."

"I know." He kisses my neck. "I think it's the bond. Or

because we're all bloodline vampires. Doesn't matter why." Each sentence is punctuated by a slow thrust. "We can scent each other on you. It makes me crazed."

I run my hands down his back and grip his ass, urging him to fuck me harder. "Give me more."

"I'll give you everything." He lifts his head and I catch the metallic scent of blood a moment before he kisses me. He nicked his tongue and his blood coats our kiss, ramping up my desire even more.

More.

I can't get enough.

I suck on his tongue as he fucks me. He shifts his angle and presses his thumb to my clit, working me until I orgasm all over his cock. I half expect him to follow me over the edge, but Malachi has other plans.

He fucks me through my orgasm, his body a cage I don't want to escape. Only as the last wave fades does he slow down, his strokes gaining a leisurely pace that curls my toes. He nips my bottom lip. "They won't be back for a while."

I dig my nails into his ass and lift my hips to take him deeper yet. "Guess we'll have to entertain ourselves."

"Guess so."

We don't stop for a very, very long time.

6

I'M IN THE KITCHEN THE NEXT DAY WHEN I FEEL IT. A sense of...not exactly wrongness, but an intrusion. I nearly drop the bowl I'm holding. "What is *that?*"

Instantly, Malachi is on alert. "What is what?"

"There's this..." I frown. "I don't know how to explain it. It's like an itch I can't scratch."

He narrows his eyes. "Where?"

Without looking, I point nearly behind me. "There. I can't tell how far."

He doesn't hesitate. "*Rylan.*" Before the sound of the other vampire's name is finishing echoing through the house, Malachi has me in his arms and he's moving in that nearly-too-fast speed, flying through the rooms and out the front door—on the opposite side of the house from where I felt the intrusion.

Rylan lands beside us, and I get the impression that he jumped from the second or third story. His dark hair is a little ruffled, but he's back to wearing a suit and looks freshly pressed. "What's going on?"

"She felt something. Coming from the opposite direction."

I expect Rylan to laugh it off. Why should he take this seriously when he barely bothers to listen to a single word that comes out of my mouth? But his gaze narrows the same way Malachi's did. "Get to the safe house we agreed on. I'll take a look and call Wolf to update him." He pulls off his jacket, quickly followed by his shirt.

I tense. "Wait. I like this house. There's no reason to run if—"

"Rylan will take a look. If he gives the signal, we'll come back." Malachi is already moving, rushing through the trees that surround the house at a pace I could never dream of matching. I have no choice but to cling to him. At this point, I'm just grateful that, for once, I was actually wearing clothing. My shorts and oversized T-shirt are hardly appropriate for the briskness of the weather, but it's better than being naked.

The cry of a giant bird reaches us, and I only need to see Malachi's face to know that it's not good news. "They found us again?"

"Looks like it." He picks up his pace, nearly flying across the uneven ground. "We'll know more after we meet up with Rylan and Wolf."

It took them less than a week to track us down this time. They're closing the gap, and no one can figure out how. Hell, if seraphim and demons exist, maybe witches do, too. Maybe they have some sort of scrying spell. I'll ask Malachi about it after we get out of danger. I don't *think* any of my father's people can match him in size, speed, and strength, but I wouldn't have wagered on my father trapping Malachi behind a blood ward for decades on end.

I could keep peppering him with questions, but the truth is that until we regroup with the others, the only priority is to put as much distance between us and the other vampires as possible. We can't fight, not without risking one of us getting hurt. There's no reasoning with them. They're following orders, and only a direct order from my father will change their course.

This is a race, but I still don't know the parameters. I know *our* goals, but we have no idea what my father knows.

I lift my head and tug on Malachi's shirt. "We need one of them alive."

He glances at me without breaking stride. "That's risky."

"I'm aware. But we need to know if he's pursuing us because he wants you back or if he knows what happened when we broke the blood ward." If he knows I have seraph blood, that I awoke that power, that I'm bonded with not one but *three* bloodline vampires...

That changes everything.

If he can get his hands on me, he'll hold the leash for three of the seven bloodlines. I know all too well the lengths he'll go to get what he wants once we're under his control. The men might be able to hold out indefinitely, but if I have to choose between keeping them alive or doing something really unforgivable, I already know what I'll choose.

My father knows that, too.

"We need to know," I repeat.

Malachi nods. He doesn't turn back, but that's fine. Getting to a secondary location is the primary goal. We know where *they're* headed, and they'll stay at the house for at least a short period of time to plumb it for any information they can. We just have to pick one of them off when they leave. It sounds easy, but I know better.

I lay my head against Malachi's chest and let him carry me away.

Judging by the position of the sun in the sky, several hours have passed by the time he slows and sets me on my feet. I study the little farmhouse in the distance. It's surrounded by rolling fields and looks like something out of a painting. "Is that where we're headed?"

"Yes." He rolls his shoulders. He doesn't look like he's been sprinting at full speed while carrying another person, but he *does* look tired. "Rylan will have gotten word to Wolf by now. They'll meet us here."

"We have to—"

"I know, little dhampir. But no one is going back there until you're secured."

As much as I want to argue, he's right. We fall into an easy jog that eats up the distance at a pace slightly faster than an athletic human could maintain. My knee barely twinges. A month ago, I wouldn't have been able to do this. Not after my father shattered my knee in punishment for an escape attempt. He wanted to make sure I'd never be able to run again, and it was a reality I'd made a tumultuous peace with. Until Malachi gave me his blood.

Bloodline vampires really are something special.

My father always set himself above the rest at the compound, and up until I met Malachi, I thought that was just narcissistic bullshit because my father has some magic. Now I realize how deeply the difference between normal vampires and bloodline vampires go.

Malachi is the last of his line, those who carry the power to control fire. If he doesn't have children, his bloodline will die with him. I glance in his direction. "Do Wolf and Rylan have family?"

He doesn't take his gaze from the farmhouse. "You mean others that are part of their bloodline? Yes. Not many, but yes."

Not many.

Guilt claws at my throat. "Shouldn't they be out procreating or something to ensure their bloodlines keep going? I understand why you didn't, but they weren't trapped behind a blood ward."

"We live very long lives, Mina. There's no rush." The words are right, but there's something off in his tone.

Once again, Wolf's words, Malachi's words come back to me. He wants me pregnant with his babies. It's still a little mindblowing. A few months ago, pregnancy wasn't even on my radar, and now it's my highest priority. Even that hardly seems real, though. My future is measured in goals right now.

Survive. Get pregnant. Become heir. Kill my father.

Every time I try to think of *after*, my brain bounces off the concept. Pregnancy is one thing. Children is something entirely different. But if I get pregnant, the *goal* is children.

"I'm going to be a terrible mother."

Malachi stops. I don't notice for two steps, not until he reaches out and snags my wrist. "Don't say that."

"It's the truth." I don't look back at him. "I don't know what your childhood was like. Maybe it's been so long that you don't really remember. I'm only twenty-five, Malachi. Those memories are still fresh and bloody in my head." My violent, manipulative father. My ghost of a mother. How does someone come from such trauma without perpetuating the cycle?

"Mina." He tugs on my wrist. When I don't turn, he tugs again, harder this time. I know I could tell him to stop and he would, but I let him haul me back to stand before him. "Look at me."

Reluctantly, I obey, lifting my gaze to his.

He catches my chin, holding me in place. "Do you want children?"

The question makes me laugh. The sound comes out almost like a sob. "What does that matter? The path is set."

"It matters."

No, it really doesn't. Not to me. I try to pull back, but he keeps me easily in place. "Malachi, please."

"Answer the question."

It's a simple question. A vital one, even. Why does it make me want to cry? I close my eyes, hiding from him as much as I'm trying to keep the burning internal. "I don't know. It was never a possibility until it was a decision thrust upon me, first by my father and then by this situation." All true, but not the full truth. My lower lip quivers despite my best efforts. If anyone else asked me this... But it's not anyone else. It's Malachi. "Maybe part of me has always wanted kids, but it was never in the cards. And now that it is—"

"This situation is hardly ideal in that respect."

His understatement makes me open my eyes. "You want kids."

"Of course I want kids." He shrugs as if this is a given. "I always have. Not simply to continue my line. I..." Malachi glances away and clenches his jaw. "I want a family."

The way he says it. Like it's a sin to be ashamed of. Maybe it is in our world, where marriages and children are political right down to their very core. There are no love matches in my father's compound, no matter what some there would like to believe. "I see."

"Maybe it's foolish to want something that so few of our people have, but I want it all the same."

I know what he means even without him explicitly saying it. "There does seem to be a dearth of happy childhoods among vampires."

"It doesn't have to be that way."

I try to picture what he's saying. A happy childhood. I've seen it represented fictionally, but a part of me always believed it to be exactly that—fiction. Even the humans manage to fuck up their kids in astronomical numbers, and most of them are attempting to marry and procreate because of love rather than politics. The odds are not in our favor.

They're especially not in our favor with this current situation.

I don't want to ask the question, but I need to know the answer. "What happens if I get pregnant and you're not the father?" Even with Rylan attempting to stay out of the race to impregnate me, Wolf and I have sex nearly as often as Malachi and I do.

He shrugs. "It doesn't matter to me. I've made my choice."

As if it's just that simple. "If we broke the bond and one of them got me pregnant instead... Malachi, you'd be free. Free for the first time in decades. You should be focusing on that instead of tying yourself to a sinking ship."

"Mina."

Gods, the way he says my name. It makes me shiver. "Yes?"

"I respect your ability to make decisions for yourself enough to stand by while Wolf courts a demon, even though I don't agree with it. Give me the courtesy of returning the favor."

I open my mouth to continue arguing, but I don't have a leg to stand on. He's right. No matter what I think, he's more than capable of making his own choices. I swallow hard. "Okay. Sorry. I just don't want you to end up regretting..."

"Regretting you." Malachi gives me a small sliver of a smile. "Impossible. You've crashed into my life with all the subtlety of a bomb detonating, but it's been refreshing." He turns us toward the farmhouse. "Now, let's get inside and discuss next steps."

And that's that.

I'm completely unsurprised to step through the door and find that Wolf and Rylan both beat us here. Neither of them were weighed down with carrying me or having that conversation out in the field before entering. That said... I glance at Wolf. "How did you know we moved?"

"Rylan caught me on the way back." He hops onto the faded counter and rubs his hands together. "I should have news on the demon front within a day or two. Those bastards like to play hard to get."

Malachi appears in the doorway. "Everything is secure."

"I told you it was." Rylan is staring out the window as if

he'd rather be anywhere but here. I can't exactly blame him, but I won't pretend that his attitude isn't grating on me. Obviously things aren't going to magically change between us just because of what happened two nights ago, but would it kill the asshole to *look* at me?

Malachi moves to lean against the counter next to Wolf. "We can't keep operating like this. The demon deal is a long shot, but even if we remove the bond, it won't remove the threat Cornelius represents. We need to know what he knows."

Finally, Rylan turns from the window. "You want to take one of his men."

"Yes."

"It won't be easy. We'll have to kill the rest of the scouting party."

"I'm aware."

I look between them. "If it's too dangerous—"

"It's not." Rylan cuts a hand through the air. "Malachi and I are more than capable of dealing with a handful of Cornelius's dogs. It will incite him to send more next time, but Malachi's right. We need the information."

Malachi crosses his arms over his large chest. "It was Mina's idea."

"I see." Rylan clenches his jaw and seems to make himself look at me. He might have an expression like he's chewing on rocks, but even he can't mask the heat in his dark eyes.

An answering heat licks through me, but I shove down the sensation. Now isn't the time, and he won't thank me for it. "The sooner we do this, the better."

7

WOLF KICKS OUT HIS HEELS AND GRABS MALACHI'S shoulder when it looks like the larger man is about to speak. "We know you don't like leaving the pretty little dhampir alone, but she won't be alone. She'll be with me."

"That's not the comfort you think it is."

Wolf laughs. "We both know I'm capable of keeping her among the living. If I'm so inclined."

"My last statement stands." Malachi sighs. "But if you lay down a blood ward, I'll consider myself comforted."

Alarm blares through me. "No. Not another blood ward." Not when one of those spells was responsible for keeping Malachi trapped in that rotting house for far too long.

"Don't worry, love. I don't know which one of my worthless cousins was greedy enough to be bribed by your father, but wards are capable of more than just containing. We can keep the enemy out with them." He makes a face. "They're not exactly fun to put in place, though, and feeding from you so soon after Rylan fucked things up is out of the question."

Rylan startles. "That's not—"

"Take the blood from me." Malachi's already turning for the door. "The faster we move on this, the better."

"You're no fun, old friend." Wolf hops off the counter. "But you know what would make it more fun?"

Malachi's sigh is fond. "We don't have time for that."

"There's always time for that."

I listen to them bicker as they move deeper into the house. Judging from the quick look I got at the layout when Malachi whisked me inside, they're heading for the living room. It's fully enclosed, without a single window, so the easiest to fortify. I hold out a hand when Rylan starts to follow them. "They've got this."

"You don't give me orders."

I bite back a sigh. "No, I don't give you orders. But they're about to fuck, and unless you're going to pull that stick out of your ass and join in, you stalking after them is going to be distracting."

Again, that tiny startle. He seems to give me his full attention. "It doesn't bother you that they're intimate when you're not around."

"Why would it? Their relationship predates me." I pause. "So does yours."

"Ancient history." But the way he glances at the doorway gives lie to his words. I don't know what happened with Malachi and Rylan. I haven't asked, and neither of them has offered.

Malachi and Wolf make more sense in my head. Theirs is a friend-ship that often includes sex, and they hold each other lightly in a way that suggests they aren't heartbroken by the years they've spent apart. As if they've come together and parted over and over again through their lives. I don't have confirmation, of course, but it's there in the way they interact.

Rylan is different.

Wolf doesn't seem to see me as a threat. I'm just another play-thing for his amusement and pleasure when he's around. Rylan looks at me as if I stole his only love.

Maybe I did.

"Rylan—"

"No." He shakes his head. "Gods, you're practically beam-ing your emotions into my brain. Stop it. I don't want or need your pity."

I close my eyes and try to shove the feeling away, grasping for something else to feel instead. Anger lingers just below the sur-face, just like it always does. I grab it with both hands and wrap it around me like a comforting blanket. When I open my eyes, he's lost that nearly feral look. "Better?"

"Barely."

I glare. "I didn't know I was projecting my emotions. Malachi only just told me before we had to run."

He shrugs, turning for the door. "It's simply another burden to bear."

That's about enough of that. I grab Rylan's arm. He's too strong to move, so when I yank, I end up pulling myself for-ward instead of him back. He jerks away from me, but I'm not in the mood to let this conversation remain unfinished. I stalk him across the kitchen, barely aware that he's retreating until I have him pressed against the counter.

Only then do I realize what I was doing.

I jerk back. "Sorry."

Rylan catches my elbows, stopping me from backing up. "You want to be a predator? Stop second-guessing yourself."

I yank, but he's holding me too firmly. "I don't want to be a predator." I pull back again. Fail again. "Not with you three."

"I don't fucking understand you." He says it so softly, I almost miss the words.

Just like that, my anger flares hot enough to scald. "Oh, because I'm not playing the part of the monster the way you want? Because I'm just as in over my head as the rest of you? Which part, Rylan? Please enlighten me so we can get past this bullshit."

"There's no getting past some things."

We're so close, we're sharing the same air. I hate that I want nothing more than to press my body against his, to claim his mouth so I can swallow down his poisonous words, can take every part of him into me until we're both a shaking mess.

I want to blame the bond for this. Surely I'm not so twisted as to desire a man who clearly hates me. Unfortunately, the truth is significantly less convenient. The bond is present, of course, but it's not pulling at me the same way it did two nights ago. I am firmly in control. Which means I have no one to blame but myself.

"Let go," I say softly. "We might not be able to control the fact that the bond requires us to drink and fuck each other, but if you really hate me as much as you say, then let me go right fucking now."

Rylan's grip spasms on my elbows. For a moment, his cold expression flickers and I get a glimpse of the feral creature within, the one more in line with the animals he can shift into than the smoothly cultured vampire he normally presents to the world. "I don't hate you."

"Could have fooled me."

He still doesn't release me. "Malachi and Wolf are too young to remember what your people did to ours, but I'm not. It's not something I can release simply because you're not acting like *they* did."

I know this. Of course I know this. He might not have said as much in so many words up to this point, but his hatred goes far too deep to be directed at me personally. I don't blame him for it. That doesn't mean I'm going to roll over for him, either. "I can't change what I am. I don't know if I can change what happened, but I'm trying."

He searches my face. "If Wolf can do what he says, the demon will demand a high cost."

"I'm aware."

Rylan shakes his head slowly. "I..." He takes a slow breath. "I don't want to see you hurt, Mina. I hate this bond, but that doesn't mean I want you dead."

"I know." And I do. If he wanted me dead, he wouldn't have been so panicked when he took too much blood. That strange, soft moment in the shower wouldn't have occurred. Knowing that doesn't excuse his shitty attitude, though. "Let me go, Rylan."

Finally, he releases me. When I don't immediately step back, his lips curl into something that's almost a smile. "If you're not opposed to the idea, I think it'd be wise to ensure the bond doesn't get to the point of desperation again."

"So formal." I tilt my head to the side. "You're saying you want to have sex again."

"Yes." The word is almost a sigh.

"Okay."

Rylan blinks. "Okay?"

"Yeah. Okay." I force myself to take a step back, and then another. "You irritate the hell out of me, and I kind of want to smack you on a regular basis, but I like fucking you, Rylan." Now it's my turn to hesitate. "However, I understand if you don't want to throw your hat into the ring, so to speak. If you want to keep things to anal or oral to avoid the risk of pregnancy, that's okay, too."

Another of those slow blinks. "I don't understand you."

"You don't have to understand me." Part of me kind of wants him to, though. I wave a hand at my body. "No matter what else is true about this bond, babies change things. I'm not going to force you."

He takes a step toward me, and some lingering prey instinct has me backing up. Rylan stalks me across the kitchen, his eyes bleeding silver, his movements going nearly feline. A bolt of heat goes through me when I remember his claws sinking into my skin. I liked that. I liked it a lot. "Rylan."

"You might be pregnant already." He pins me to the counter, the mirror image to what I just did to him. Except he doesn't preserve that last little bit of distance between us. His hips meet mine, and there's no ignoring his hard cock. "It will be weeks before we know."

"Honestly, with the timeline, it's likely to be less than a week." I had my period right after we went on the run, and I tend to be regular.

He leans down and drags his nose over my throat. Directly against the spot he bit me two nights ago. "No reason to deny myself then. Not until we know."

My hands find his chest, but I'm not sure if I'm trying to push him back or pull him closer. "That's faulty logic," I manage.

"I can live with it." He leans back a little. "Can you?"

I shouldn't. No matter how much I desire this vampire, the fact remains that he's got a boatload of baggage when it comes to the seraphim. He didn't choose this bond, and he resents it more than the other two combined. Throwing a child into the mix is a recipe for disaster.

And yet.

And yet I can't stop myself from sliding my hands down his stomach to the front of his slacks. "We shouldn't."

His hands brush my hips and then my shorts and panties fall down my legs in ragged tatters. I jolt and then whimper at the sight of his claws. "Why didn't your claws come out that first time?"

"I didn't lose control then."

My hands shake as I undo his slacks and pull out his cock. "Why are you losing control, Rylan?" I can't tell if I'm trying to taunt him or legitimately asking the question.

"You make me crazed." He digs his hands into my hair and then his mouth is on mine. It's no less vicious a kiss than it was last time, with the bond riding us so hard. The knowledge thrills me even as I get up onto my tiptoes to press closer to him. Knowing that this untamed version of Rylan lurks beneath his icy exterior drives me wild.

He hooks my thighs, his claws dragging across my skin, and lifts me onto the counter. "Can't bite you," he mutters. I barely have time to brace before he goes to his knees and covers my pussy with his mouth. He's just as unrestrained in this as he was in the kiss. I slam back against the cabinets with a moan.

Rylan spears my pussy with his tongue and I freeze at the feeling of it...growing. I stare down at him. "Rylan," I moan.

He fucks me with his tongue, a wicked look in his silver eyes. He knows exactly what he's doing to me, and he's getting off on it nearly as hard as I am. The sheer wickedness of knowing that he's shifting parts of his body while inside me has me sinking my hands into his hair as best I can and lifting my hips to fuck his tongue. "Please."

He moves up to my clit, working me in expert strokes. My toes curl and heat licks through me. I'm dancing on the edge of a truly spectacular orgasm when he shoves to his feet and presses his cock to my entrance. I can't be sure, but I think he might be bigger than last time. His claws dig into the counter as he wedges himself into me in short strokes.

"More." I grab his wrists and he lets me pry his hands off the counter and put them on my hips. "I like your marks on me."

Rylan freezes. A shudder works its way through his body,

and when he speaks, he sounds like an entirely different person. "*Fuck.*"

He jerks me forward, impaling me on his cock, and then his arms are around me. Pain sparks on my ass and a twin prick on the back of my neck. He's holding me entirely off the counter as he drives into me. Deeper and deeper, until it's almost too much and yet not enough.

My earlier near orgasm roars up and sweeps me under. I cling to him as I come, loving the pain as much as I love the pleasure. He thrusts into me almost brutally, only his hold on the back of my neck keeping my head from bashing against the cabinets. "More."

"Take it," I gasp.

And then he's kissing me, claiming my mouth with his tongue the same way his cock is claiming my pussy. He growls against my lips. It's the only warning I get before he orgasms, pumping me full of his come. I swear I can actually feel it inside me, but it must be my imagination.

Rylan nips my bottom lip and shifts to the side to drag his tongue up the side of my neck. Licking the blood from my skin. There's a tiny spark and I know he's healing me with his nicked tongue. I shiver. The urge rises to say something, but I don't know what words to bring forth that won't send us hurtling back into icy anger.

I hold perfectly still as he leans back. He looks down our bodies and watches his cock ease out of me, his expression strange. "Let's get you some clothes."

So we're just...not going to talk about it?

Works for me.

"I didn't have a chance to bring anything." I hop off the counter, and my legs go a little funny.

"I know." He grabs my elbow. Rylan doesn't sweep me into his arms the way Malachi would in this situation. He doesn't make any sly comments like Wolf would. He simply waits for me to find my legs and releases me.

I follow him in the opposite direction Malachi and Wolf went, to the back of the house where the bedrooms apparently are. Rylan pulls out a dress from one of the closets and passes it to me. It's not necessarily something I would have chosen for myself—a floral sundress that reminds me entirely too much of the one I wore that first night I walked into Malachi's home, soaked to the bone and filled to the brim with rage and fear. So much has changed since then and yet so little at the same time. It's not a comfortable realization.

I waste no time pulling off my shirt and tugging the sundress on. It fits perfectly, which just goes further to confirm my suspicion that one of them has been going ahead of us and supplying these safe houses. Every one we've ended up in has clothing that at least mostly fits us as well as food for me.

It's only when I'm buttoning up the front of it that I realize Rylan is still watching me. "What?"

"Nothing." He doesn't turn away, though. "I keep waiting for this attraction to wear off, but it only seems to be getting stronger. It's damned inconvenient."

I laugh. It's the only proper response to that understatement of the century. I run my fingers through my hair. I don't think he got any blood on it. "If it makes you feel better, I don't like you most of the time, but I want you, too."

"Strangely enough, it does." He gives me one of those razor-thin smiles. "Let's check on the others."

I don't have to check on them to know what they're doing. Wolf never hesitates to bring sex into any given situation, and Malachi might pretend that he's the controlled one, but it's plain to anyone who spends time in their presence for ten seconds that he missed the other vampire. "They're fucking by now."

Rylan stops in the doorway. "I know."

I should leave it alone, but I wouldn't be me if I wasn't pushing. "Both of them would be thrilled if you joined in."

His shoulders drop the barest amount. "I know that, too."

I don't ask him why he's holding out. We have enough to deal with without me meddling in affairs that started centuries before I was born. I can't help wanting to smooth things over and give these three vampires what little happiness we can find in this world.

It's not my place.

Apparently I *am* capable of restraint.

I motion to the door. "After you."

8

The blood barrier feels strange.

I couldn't feel the one around Malachi's house. I passed over it without even being aware it existed. This is different. I'm not sure if it's because my seraph power has awakened or if it's the barrier itself.

I reach out, startled to discover the air feeling like it gets thicker the closer my palm comes to the doorway into the living room. "Weird."

"Stop." Rylan catches my wrist. "Don't touch it until he lets you in. Knowing Wolf, there will be some nasty surprise if you do."

Through the doorway, we can see Malachi and Wolf. They've lost their clothes somewhere along the way and Malachi is covered in blood. Their bodies move in a rhythm as old as time itself, Malachi thrusting into Wolf and Wolf rising to meet him.

Despite the orgasm I just had, desire heats my blood as I watch. "They're so damn beautiful."

"Yes."

The pain in Rylan's voice drags my attention to him. He looks agonized, so much so that he's forgotten to wear his normal icy mask. It hurts my chest and I rub my hand against my sternum. I don't know how to fix this. I don't even know where to begin. He won't thank me for meddling, either.

When there are no right answers, I go with the only tool at my disposal.

I sink to my knees before him. He tracks the movement. "What are you doing?"

Relying entirely on instinct. I run a single finger along the hard length of his cock where it presses against his slacks. "May I?"

"Mina." He shudders out a breath. "Yes."

I carefully undo his slacks and draw out his cock. Fucking Rylan is one thing. I know I can take most of what he can give me. Giving him head when he might lose control is something else altogether. I'm particularly vulnerable like this. If he shifts or...

It doesn't matter.

Right now, he needs me and I refuse to back away from that need. I hold his gaze and take his cock into my mouth as best I can. Even without partially shifting, he's still large enough that my jaw aches. I push the pain away and hold his gaze, taking him deeper.

His eyes flash silver and he reaches for me before he seems to catch himself. Likely he's all too aware of what his claws could do to my face if he forgets himself.

I withdraw slowly and rub my lips against his blunt head. "Watch them."

"*Fuck*." Rylan's back hits the wall behind him and he stabs his claws into the drywall. But he does as I say and lifts his gaze to watch the two vampires fucking on the other side of the doorway.

I go back to sucking his cock. He's shaking with the strength of his restraint, and while I appreciate it, a reckless part of me wants that uncontrolled edge he keeps showing me. I crave it on a level I'm not prepared to deal with.

His length prevents me from taking him entirely, so I use my hands to compensate, focusing every bit of my attention on making him feel good. If I can give him nothing else, I can do this. Pleasure. It won't balance the scales of the bond or the mess we're in, but it's something.

Rylan starts thrusting. At first, it's so subtle, I barely notice his hips rising to meet my lips on each downstroke. But all too quickly, he's fucking my mouth. I can tell he's still being careful, still too aware of how much larger and stronger he is.

I look up and pause when I find him watching *me* instead of Malachi and Wolf. We stare at each other and I see the exact moment he snaps. He grabs a fistful of my hair and pulls me off his cock, shoving me to the floor and covering me with his body. And then he's inside me and, gods, I don't know how it keeps being this good.

With Rylan, it isn't sex.

It isn't even fucking.

It's *rutting*.

He thrusts into me so hard, we inch our way up the hallway

toward the living room. Rylan glances up and snarls. He drags one nail down his throat, leaving a long line of blood that makes my mouth water. Then he sinks his claws into the wood floor on either side of my hips, pinning me in place as he fucks me.

I arch up and close my mouth around his throat. The first swallow of blood sizzles through my veins. The second sweeps me away entirely. Pleasure and pain and power. I never knew it could be like this, never knew that I could have anything but pain.

I come hard, so hard that I forget myself and bite his neck. It doesn't matter that I don't have fangs like a vampire. I'm acting on instinct alone.

Rylan curses and then he's grinding into me as he comes. Filling me up again.

I hope he doesn't regret this.

The thought feels as wispy as smoke, wafting away before I can grasp it fully. The sound of footsteps makes me shift to look over our heads. Malachi stands in the doorway, gloriously naked, watching us with a look that I can only describe as possessive. Like we're both his and he's pleased that we've finally gotten out of our own way and closed the circle. Maybe it's my imagination, but I don't think so.

Rylan moves back and climbs carefully to his feet, pulling me up with him. It takes a few seconds to get our clothing back in order, but he doesn't say a word and I'm not about to be the one to break this particular silence.

Malachi nods. "I need to get dressed and then we'll go. Mina, stay with Wolf. He'll protect you." He pulls me into his arms and kisses me. I barely get a chance to sink into it before he's stepping back. "We'll have information when we return."

"Be safe." I try to smile at him and then look at Rylan. "Both of you."

They nod, and then they're gone, disappearing into the growing darkness of the house. I don't think the sun has quite set yet, but it's hard to say without windows to look through. I turn to find Wolf lounging in the doorway. He's pulled on pants, but only barely. They're not fastened and cling precariously to his narrow hips, as if one wrong move will send them sliding down his legs.

He grins. "'Twas Beauty who tamed the beast."

"Oh hush." I eye the blood ward. "Is this going to fry me?"

"Not with an invitation." He reaches through, his hand an elegant offering. "Come here, love. We have things to discuss."

I lay my hand in his and let him pull me through the ward. It sizzles a little against my skin in a way that isn't entirely comfortable, but it doesn't hurt. I touch my lips. "My father's ward didn't feel like that."

"It was keyed to keep Malachi in, not other people out." He shrugs and pulls me to the couch. "Now, be a good girl and keep quiet while the adults are talking."

I frown. I don't know what's going on, but it can't be positive. I dig in my heels, for all the good it does me. He just drags me the rest of the way and half tosses me onto the couch. "What's going on?"

"We're going to have some *fun*." Wolf throws himself down next to me and pulls me against his body. "You wanted to meet a demon, yes?"

Oh no.

I start to sit up, but he catches my shoulder and tucks me back against him. "Wolf, you can't. Not without Malachi."

"Malachi might pass for the leader of our little group, but he won't let you make a deal, no matter what's offered." His eerie blue eyes watch me closely. "Do you deny it?"

I open my mouth to do just that, but I can't. Not without lying. "He's overprotective."

"Exactly."

"I thought you said it'd be a couple days before we are able to make contact."

"I lied." He dips a finger beneath the strap of my sundress, tracing a line down to my breast. He circles my nipple. "It's a shame we don't have time. Soon."

"Wolf—"

The air changes in the room. I don't know how to explain it. It doesn't go cold or hot or anything like that. There's no buzz of electricity like when Wolf brought me through the barrier. It's more like an...aura of danger. Every prey instinct I have demands I go still and silent and hope the predator that just entered the room moves on without noticing me.

"Good girl," Wolf murmurs. He still hasn't taken his hand from my sundress, his middle finger idly tracing my nipple.

A few feet in front of us, in the middle of the room, the shadows gather. They seem to gain weight and height in a way normal shadows most definitely do *not* do. A masculine voice emerges, deep and as decadent as dark chocolate. "It's been a long time, Wolf."

"You always were one for theatrics." Wolf leans back, taking me with him, and crosses his ankle over his knee. "I'm not one of your pretty, desperate women. You don't have to do the whole song and dance with me."

"And yet you have a pretty woman with you." The darkness fades slowly, revealing a man. Except he'd only be mistaken for a normal man if someone didn't have an ounce of self-preservation or a single instinct to their name. Light brown skin, dark hair and eyes, a face so perfect it's actually a little eerie to look at. He catches me staring and smiles.

I flinch. Yes, he might be pretty, but he's easily the most dangerous being I've ever come across. And that's saying something considering the men currently sharing my bed.

The demon doesn't move, but he seems closer all the same. "Or not a woman at all." He inhales slowly and his smile widens. "Seraph. Wolf, things truly are never boring when you're involved."

"What can I say? I'm a gift."

"You are." The demon studies me. It feels like he's crawling around inside my skin. "I thought you smarter than getting snagged by a seraph bond."

Wolf shrugs. He finally takes his hand from my breast and moves it to my shoulder. A reminder to stay in place. "Can you blame me?"

"With this pretty package?" The demon shrugs. "I understand, even if I wouldn't make the same misstep."

Wolf laughs, his high and wild cackle. "Liar. We both know there's one pretty little thing that's turned you into a teddy bear. How are things going on that front, Azazel?"

Just like that, the easiness is gone from the demon's face. "Watch your tongue, vampire. You amuse me, so I come when you call. The moment you stop amusing me, I'll rip your bones from your body, one by one. I'd like to see you heal from *that*."

"Yes, yes, consider me cowed." Wolf waves that away. "Can you do anything about a seraph bond?"

Azazel goes back to studying me. "If I may?"

"By all means." Wolf answers before I can do it myself.

That's all the warning I get before he's in front of me, pressing a cold hand to the center of my chest, right where I feel the bond the strongest. It's not a welcome touch, but he's hardly being untoward. At least on the surface. Beneath the surface is another thing entirely. I can feel his power course into me, thick and smooth. It leaves a prickly taste on the back of my tongue and I flinch.

Azazel moves back slowly, expression contemplative. "I can break it."

"Really?" I don't mean to speak, but I honestly didn't think he'd be able to.

He flashes me a smile that's all charm and no little amount of threat. "Human religion might be more fiction than truth, but they weren't wrong on this one subject. Demons and seraphim are natural enemies, and our powers reflect that. I can dig out a seraph bond."

Wolf narrows his eyes. "Would that mean seraphs can negate demon deals?"

"Careful, vampire. You're playing with fire again."

"Silly me." Wolf tucks me more firmly against his side. "Let's hear it. All the nitty-gritty details."

Azazel is still studying me. "It's not likely to kill the vampires involved, though that's always a possible side effect." He shrugs. "I like you, Wolf, so the cost is my normal rate. Seven years of service."

I open my mouth, but Wolf beats me there. "We'll consider it. You'll have the answer within a week."

"Normally, there's little rush, but I have a pressing engagement in ten days." Azazel gives that dangerous smile again. "Having a seraph on the auction block would be quite the feather in my cap. The others would love it."

"You'll have the answer within the week," Wolf repeats, an edge in his voice.

"So be it." Azazel shrugs and then he is gone, disappearing in a surge of shadows. It takes several long minutes before all remnants of his power dissipate as well.

Only then does Wolf release me and sigh. "Well, that's a dead end."

"What? Seven years isn't that long." Even if I'm not immortal—something I still need to investigate—I'm going to live significantly longer than a human would. Seven years is nothing if it means breaking the bond.

"Here's a hint, love. If it sounds too good to be true, it almost certainly is." Wolf leans his head against the back of the couch and closes his eyes. "Azazel says seven years, but he's not talking about in the mortal realm. He's talking about in the demon realm. That might mean a few seconds gone here, or it might be a few hundred years. There's no way to tell, and he'll lie if you ask him. The way the realms interact when it comes to time passing is one of the few things Azazel's deals can't control."

Panic flickers through me, but I shove it down. "So a few hundred years pass. Who cares? It's not as if I have any ties to this...realm." Later, I'll have a mental breakdown about the fact that there is apparently more than one realm. Right now, compartmentalizing is the name of the game. "You'll all still be alive."

"Maybe." Wolf stares intently at the spot where Azazel disappeared. "But if he's auctioning you off..." He shakes his head. "Malachi would go nuclear. Rylan might be more subtle about it, but he's not going to let you auction off that pretty pussy for his sake."

"What about you?" I don't mean to ask the question. I really don't. But it's out in the air between us, and there's no taking it back.

"What about me?" Wolf grabs one of my thighs and tugs it up and over his lap. He skates his hand up beneath my dress and palms my bare pussy. "I'm a horrible cliché, love. I'm not overly fond of the thought of you fucking any monsters but us."

"But..." My thoughts scatter as he pushes two fingers into me. "But, Wolf." It's nearly impossible to focus while he's slowly fucking me with his fingers, that hungry look on his face, but I give it a valiant effort. "But the bond."

"Eh." He pulls his fingers out to spread my wetness up and around my clit. "No matter how much it triggers Rylan, you're hardly an evil overlord." He uses his thumb to stroke my clit. "If that ever changes, I'll kill you myself."

9

Maybe I should find the threat of Wolf killing me terrifying. Wolf *is* terrifying. Even knowing him such a short time, I'm painfully aware of the fact that he doesn't bluff. It doesn't make him more predictable, though. He changes direction as easily as the wind.

Still...

"Promise me."

He pauses, his dark brows pulling together. "What?"

"Promise me that you'll kill me if I try to abuse the bond."

He lets loose one of those mad laughs that I've come to enjoy so much. "No. I don't make promises I don't intend to keep."

"But—"

"What if you abuse the bond on accident, baby seraph?" He goes back to slowly fucking me with his fingers, his thumb playing across my clit. "It would be a shame if I had to rip out your throat because of an ill-worded promise. Malachi would never forgive me."

"Can't have that," I say faintly.

"Now you get the idea." He topples me back onto the couch and settles between my thighs. "Ah, this brings back memories."

From the first time we met. I try to glare, but it's half-hearted at best. "You mean when you held me down and drank my blood a few minutes after meeting me?"

Wolf chuckles. "You mean when Malachi extended guest privileges and it infuriated you so much, you welcomed my bite and the ensuing orgasm."

He has me there. I was *furious*. "You would have fucked me then if I gave you half a chance."

"Of course." He lifts himself off me enough to undo his pants and work them down his hips. "Just like I'm going to fuck you now. For old times' sake."

"Uh-huh."

He tugs down my sundress, baring my breasts. "You really are exquisite, love. Perfect breasts. A pussy that's enough to have a partner willing to cage you for eternity." He palms my breasts, lingering over my nipples. "The demon deal is off the table."

"You don't get to make that decision." I arch into his palms. It feels good, but it's nowhere near enough. "I need you."

Wolf wraps a fist around his cock and guides it to my entrance. "This is exactly why. Do you know what kind of monsters they have in the demon realm, love?"

"I didn't know the demon realm existed until an hour ago."

His laugh is a little strained. He's moving slowly, teasing me, sinking inch by inch deeper. "They make us vampires look like house cats. They'll get one taste, one touch of this pussy, and they'll chain you up and never let you go."

I reach down to grab his hips even as I lift mine to take him deeper. "My choice to make, Wolf."

"I'm not a jealous man." He surges forward, sheathing himself inside me completely, and moves down to press his entire body to mine. "I'm not."

I can barely think past how good it feels to have him inside me, but I give it a valiant effort. "Say it again and you might even believe it."

He shifts down a little and bites me. His teeth sink into the curve of my breast. Not a spot where he's going to get much blood, but the effect is overwhelming. I release his hips and grab his head, guiding him to my nipple. "Again."

"Must be the bond," he mutters. "I want to mark you up. Rub my scent all over you." His hands find the spots where Rylan held me down earlier, at my neck and back. "Mark you just like Rylan did. Just like Malachi wants to."

I guide him to my other breast. "Do it."

He does. Again and again and again. Tiny little bites that ramp up my pleasure. Looking down my body and seeing little rivulets of blood marking my skin do just as much for me as the bites themselves. I *love* these marks just as much as I love the ones from Rylan's claws. A sign of mutual ownership, of them claiming me the same way the bond demands I claim them.

Later, I'll worry this is some sort of magic. Right now, there's no room for anything but the feeling of Wolf's little bites in time with his cock sliding in and out of me. Need winds tighter and tighter, arching my body and drawing a cry from my lips. "More!"

He gives me more. Even so, he's not rushing. Time ceases to have meaning as we fuck, our bodies moving in a rhythm as familiar as breathing. With each wave of pleasure, my orgasm edges closer, stronger. When he finally loops his arm under my waist and lifts my hips to find the sensitive spot inside me with each stroke, I lose control completely. I grab his arms and scream. I think I might even black out. All I know is one moment I'm coming so hard the room goes black, and the next I'm blinking up into Wolf's crimson eyes as he finishes inside me.

I'm so dazed, I almost miss the low word he utters. "*Ours.*" A promise and a threat.

The sweat is still cooling on my body when I sense the approach of Rylan and Malachi. They're moving quickly. I don't know what's changed with the bond in the last few days, but I can feel the distance closing in great detail. "They're coming."

"About time. Really, how hard is it to find a group of unsuspecting vampires, kill all but one, and then indulge in a little torture until he tells you everything he knows?" Wolf climbs to his feet and stretches his arms over his head. Even after all the fucking, the sight of him makes my body clench. I try to push the desire down, but from the way his lips pull into a seductive smile, I fail miserably.

I sit up and try to ignore the way his cock is going hard again. "Malachi told me that you can sense my emotions."

"Oh, that." He shrugs. "I don't need magic to know you want my cock again, love. It's called being perceptive."

"I need to learn how to shield."

"Why?"

I blink. "What do you mean, *why?*"

"Exactly what I said." He wraps a fist around his cock and gives a few slow pumps. "Did you ever stop to ask what the purpose of such a side effect could be?"

I start to snap, but it's rare that Wolf decides to go into teaching mode. He prefers to mock and incite instead. I cross my arms over my chest. "No, I didn't worry about why. The fact that it exists is enough for me. I don't need all three of you in my head."

"Ah, but we're not in your head." He grabs my hand and tugs me to my feet. "We're in your heart, and that's something altogether different."

"Don't talk in riddles. I don't have the patience for it."

"Pity." He laughs. Wolf dips down and licks the blood from my upper chest. The sound he makes is nearly a purr. "We're not just eager and willing cocks, love."

"One could argue that Rylan is neither eager nor willing."

He drags a single fingertip over my hip where there's still the slightest pinprick mark from Rylan's claws. It's honestly astounding that they haven't healed fully yet. I've taken blood from all three of them since then, and nothing heals quicker than vampire blood. I wonder if there's something in his claws that slows regeneration—

"Rylan didn't lose control because he hated the feeling of being inside you." He chuckles. "Did you know that when he was younger, he was wilder?"

"I thought he's significantly older than both you and Malachi."

"He is." Wolf shrugs. "But he didn't get that stick up his ass until a little over a century ago."

It doesn't take a genius to put the puzzle pieces together. If I have my dates right, that's around the time of his falling-out with Malachi and Wolf. "What does that have to do with anything?"

"He used to be wilder," he repeats and gives a happy sigh. "We had so much sex, love. The three of us and others we invited in. It was a wonderfully endless bacchanal for years."

"Again, what does that have to do with anything?"

His grin goes wide and sinful. "In all those years, I only saw him lose control of his shape when he was with Malachi and me. Only us. Never when someone else was involved."

Something goes strange in my chest, but I don't know enough to identify the emotion. "That doesn't mean anything."

"Doesn't it?" Another of those careless shrugs. "If you say so."

Malachi and Rylan are almost to the house, which is almost enough to distract me from how this conversation has gone off the rails. "Why shouldn't I learn to shield, Wolf?"

"Oh. That." He palms my breasts. "It's a protective measure."

"Excuse me?"

"When you have strong emotional spikes, all three of us feel it. Knowing when you're afraid or angry is incredibly useful on that note."

Part of me can see his point, but I'm not willing to concede. "Maybe if you chose it. You didn't, so it's invasive as hell."

"Probably." He slides his hands down my sides, his fingers unerringly finding the spots where Rylan impaled me. "Doesn't mean it's not useful. We've got to keep you alive and all that."

"Wolf—"

Movement on the other side of the blood ward. Malachi and

Rylan appear. They're covered in blood and look like something out of a horror movie. I gasp, but Wolf tightens his grip, holding me in place. "Took you long enough."

Malachi lifts his hand. The air wavers a little in front of his palm, and he recoils. "What is this, Wolf? Let us in."

"What's the password?"

"*Wolf.*"

He continues to hold me immobile, his handsome face contemplative. "It occurs to me that you two could have been taken by Cornelius. His bloodline power is glamour, after all. It would be child's play to mimic your bodies and voices and come back here to attack us."

All that is true, but it doesn't account for the fact that I *know* it's them. I grab his wrists and squeeze. "It's them. My father might be able to fool our senses, but he can't fool the bond."

He grins like I'm a student who's said something impressive. "Exactly. It's almost as if the bond does have its uses."

Damn it, I walked right into that. "Even if it does, I'm still going to learn to shield."

"That's up for debate." He finally releases me and snaps his fingers. I feel the moment the blood ward goes down. It's almost like a popping in my ears, strange but not uncomfortable.

Malachi stumbles a little as he steps into the room and true panic takes wing inside me. I push Wolf's hands away and tug my dress back into place. "You're hurt."

"I'm fine." Malachi's actions give lie to his words as Rylan ducks beneath his arm and takes the weight of the bigger vampire. "They were more prepared than we expected."

"My father is a monster, but he's no fool."

"Yes. Which means we need to move and quickly. The more distance we put between the group we just removed and the hounds he'll send next, the better." He looks around the living room as if seeing it for the first time. "What's that smell?"

"Brimstone." Rylan makes a sound suspiciously close to a snarl. "What did you do, Wolf?"

"Who, me?" Wolf pulls on his pants slowly. "I'm sure I have no idea what you're speaking of."

Both Rylan and Malachi go still. Malachi tries to straighten, but he tips to the side and Rylan has to catch him before he falls. I rush to them. "You need blood."

"I'm fine."

"You're about to take a nonconsensual nap, and you just said we need to run." I glance at Rylan. "Please put him on the couch."

For once, Rylan does what I ask without arguing. He guides Malachi to the couch and eases him down. After the briefest hesitations while I figure out the best way to do this, I simply climb into his lap and pull my hair off one side of my neck. "Drink."

"You almost died two nights ago. I'm not drinking from you right now."

"Malachi, shut up and drink." I dig my hands into his hair and guide his face to my throat. It's a token of how injured he is that he doesn't fight me. I flinch a little as his teeth sink into my skin, but then there's only pleasure.

Damn it, for once, it would be really nice if I didn't have a wave of sheer desire overwhelm me at one of their bites. It's useful most of the time, but I can hear Rylan and Wolf conversing quietly behind me, and I desperately want to know what they're saying.

I might as well try to grasp the wind with my bare hands.

With every pull of Malachi's mouth, heat courses through my body. My breasts go heavy and sensitive. My pussy throbs in time with the racing of my heart. Despite my best intentions, I rock against Malachi's hardening cock. He responds by pulling me closer. It's what I need, and yet it's also keeping me from what I need. With us pressed this tightly together, I can't reach down to the front of his pants.

It doesn't matter. I'll orgasm regardless. I'm already halfway there simply from his bite alone. That doesn't change the frustration that blooms. I want him inside me.

I want them all inside me.

The voice hardly sounds like mine, but I can't blame the desire on anyone but myself. I had all three of these vampires only once and it changed the course of my life forever. No matter what else is true, I crave that level of letting go again. The pleasure that overwhelmed me and awoke my powers.

Malachi shifts and growls against my skin, and that's all I need. I orgasm hard, whimpering and shaking and grinding against him. He lifts his head almost reluctantly and drags his tongue over the wounds his teeth left behind. A little spark of lightning against my skin lets me know that he's healed me. He shifts back to kiss me, a slow lingering greeting as if we have all the time in the world.

Rylan curses. "We have to go. Now." His voice goes low and dangerous. "We'll discuss the *demon* once we get somewhere safe."

Just like that, Malachi isn't kissing me any longer. He leans back, his expression carefully neutral. "What did you do, little dhampir?"

10

"WE'LL TALK ABOUT IT LATER—ABOUT ALL OF IT LATER. Right now we need to move." Rylan plucks me off Malachi's lap, gives my bloody front an exasperated look, and fixes my dress again.

I consider objecting that I'm not a doll to be moved around, but I also don't want to have the demon deal conversation right now. If we need to move, then we need to *move*. Talking now just means we'll be arguing for hours.

Rylan also shrugs out of his jacket and wraps it around me. "I'll carry you."

"Actually—"

"Wolf, I know you're not planning on arguing with me after you just went behind both our backs with this demon. Shut your fucking mouth."

For once, Wolf shuts his fucking mouth. He hauls Malachi

up, and the bigger vampire looks much steadier on his feet. Not happy, but steadier.

Rylan shoves a hand through his hair. "Colorado. The house in the mountains."

Wolf jolts. "That's a long run."

"We don't have a choice. It's the easiest to secure, and we need time to plan. Jumping states should give us a little more time."

He doesn't seem convinced. "They've found us at each place. It doesn't matter how many layers of subterfuge the properties are hidden beneath; they're able to link it back to us every time."

"They won't find this one. Not with who owns it."

I frown. "Why?"

"This house is owned by a friend," Rylan says. He scoops me into his arms. "We won't travel the whole way on foot." Without another word, he makes for the door. Apparently he's of the same mind as I am; we need to move now and argue later.

He breaks into a run the second we leave the house. As tempting as it is to ask about what they learned from my father's people, I force myself to be patient. It's better to get it all out at once. Maybe when we reach the car...

But no one seems interested in talking once we reach the nondescript black truck waiting behind a gas station. Since Wolf and I are the smallest of the four, we climb into the back seat, and Rylan takes the wheel. Despite my best efforts, the events of the last couple days catch up with me. I lean my head against the cool glass and close my eyes, letting the icy silence roll over me. Sleep follows on its heels and drags me under.

Dawn is creeping over the sky when I open my eyes again. I'm lying down across the seat, my head in Wolf's lap. He's got his eyes closed, though I can't tell if he's actually sleeping. Vampires *do* need sleep, albeit significantly less than humans or dhampirs. Bloodline vampires even less so. That said, I can't remember the last time I've seen any of them catch more than an hour or two. Surely we're all reaching our limits.

Maybe that's why we're headed up the mountain to this place that belongs to a friend of Rylan's.

Wolf shifts his hand to my hair without opening his eyes. "We're almost there."

As tempting as it is to stay in this position and enjoy being casually touched by Wolf, curiosity is more powerful. I sit up and look out the window.

It's like another world.

We're on a narrow road, winding our way ever upward. On either side of us, the banks veer sharply down into canyons. Really, there's barely room for our truck. If we see an oncoming vehicle, I'm not sure how we'll navigate it without someone sliding off the road.

"This is the only road in and out," Rylan says quietly. "The land is difficult terrain, even for vampires. You sensed your father's people before anyone else did."

My skin heats in something akin to embarrassment. "I don't know how I did it. I'm half-sure I imagined it."

"You didn't." This from Malachi. "We would have escaped safely, but your awareness gave us extra time."

"I don't know if I can replicate it." If they're putting their faith in me... As much as I crave being an equal part of this four-some, the reality is that for all my supposed power, I'm still doing the equivalent of learning how to walk. Some things I seem to be able to do on instinct, but that will only get me so far. "I don't want to risk all our lives on the assumption that I can recreate something I don't know how I did in the first place."

"It will be fine." Malachi sounds so damn sure, I kind of want to smack him. How dare he put so much unearned faith in me? If something happens to one of them because of it, I'll never forgive myself.

I don't get a chance to continue arguing because we round a bend and the house comes into view. House. The very term is laughable. It looks like a bunker built into the side of the mountain.

I squint. There are a handful of windows shining in the early morning sunlight, but even so, it's difficult to tell where the house ends and the mountain begins. "What is this place?"

"It's safe. That's the bottom line."

Rylan's answer isn't much of an answer, but I suppose the relative safety is all that matters. *I wonder if it protects against demons.* The thought almost makes me laugh.

Rylan guides the truck to a cleverly hidden garage door that slides open to allow us in. When we drive through, the entire car is encased in darkness as the door shuts again. Rylan mutters something and then a low light flickers to life around the perimeter of the floor. It slowly gets brighter until I can see clearly. I pick out half a dozen vehicles, ranging from luxury cars that must be horrifically expensive to something that might get mistaken for a military tank. "Interesting friend you have."

"You could say that." We pile out of the truck and Rylan leads the way to the thick metal door. He keys in a code and the light flashes green. "We'll go over security when we get settled."

Inside, I expect something that feels military and spartan, but the door opens into a charming hallway with fountains running the length of it that give the impression of gentle waterfalls. The next door opens into a small room with several more doors. The thick rug swallows my footsteps and the furniture is all high-end, but even I can see the advantage of the layout. Anyone coming in through the garage will be funneled into this room, which is a death trap. There's no room to spread out, no room for tactical advantage for the advancing enemy. Rylan ignores the two doors on the right and leads us left.

Another long hall, another small room with a series of doors.

We do this three more times before we end up in a cozy living room with a giant fireplace and comfortably sturdy furniture. He motions around us. "This is the east wing. While I realize it's not ideal to be in the one without windows, it's safer than the west wing."

"How deep are we?" I look at the ceiling, but it looks like any other ceiling in a nice, if expensive, home. There's no sensation to suggest the press of earth, the weight of a mountain over the top of us.

"Deep enough that we don't have to worry about someone trying to burrow here. It's pure rock around us, so short of dynamite, it's impenetrable. And we'll hear dynamite before they ever get close enough to be a danger."

It really is a bunker.

"The bedrooms and kitchen are through there." He waves at the doors on the other side of the room. "We need to get cleaned up and feed Mina and then we'll talk."

Wolf stretches, his spine cracking loud enough to set my teeth on edge. "Slow down there, Alpha. There's only one leader I accept in this merry little trio, and it's not you."

Trio?

Does that mean I'm outside the hierarchy? I don't know how to feel about that. Then again, I don't know how to feel about a lot that's happened since awakening my power. Why should this be any different?

Malachi shakes his head. "He's right. We're covered in blood and Mina hasn't eaten in…" He glances at me. "When?"

Damn, I was hoping he wouldn't ask me. "I don't remember."

"Thought so." He hooks an arm around my waist and half carries me to the center door. It leads into a room just as luxuriously appointed as the rest of this place. The bed is low to the ground and massive enough to fit several vampires Malachi's size. An open doorway leads into the bathroom. There's another of those clever waterfall walls and a shower with more shower heads than I can begin to know what to do with.

I brace myself for an argument. He's clearly not happy with me; he hasn't been happy with me since they identified the scent of brimstone and realized what Wolf and I have done. But Malachi just turns on the water and faces me. "Are you okay?"

"Yes." It's even the truth. I'm exhausted despite my nap in the car and my stomach is attempting to chew its way through my spine, but I'm as well as can be expected at this point. "Are you?"

He shrugs. "Things were a little more complicated than we expected, but we got the job done." He pulls me beneath the water and sets about washing me with the minty soap available. I almost argue that I'm more than capable of washing myself, but there's a fine tremor to Malachi's touch. I don't know if it's rage, lingering fear for my safety, or simply a faltering control, but I keep silent all the same. Especially since each pass of his hands over my skin seems to calm him. No doubt it's more side effects of the bond.

When we're both clean, Malachi leans down and presses his forehead to mine. "Don't do that again."

"Malachi—"

He keeps going before I can figure out what I'm trying to say. "Don't endanger yourself. Not on our behalf."

"Who says it was on your behalf? Maybe I did it so *I* could rid myself of the bond."

"Mina. Little dhampir." He leans back enough that he can hold my gaze. "It will happen again. Even if you manage to break it this time, the bond is part of being a seraph. I'm not leaving you. I'll just end up bonded to you again."

"No." I try to jerk back, but he tightens his grasp just enough to keep me in place.

"You can't run from this."

"Then I just won't fuck vampires. Simple solution." It's not simple and it's not feasible, though. Not if I want to be heir and dispose of my father. Playing vampire politics will be challenging enough with a strong partner at my side. Alone? It's just adding another layer of complications to the mix because they'll vie for a place in my bed and resent me when I don't give it to anyone.

Another trap.

Another choice, taken away.

I drag in a breath. "Please stop pushing me. I'm doing the best I can."

"I know." He wraps his arms around me and hugs me close. "I don't say this to hurt you, little dhampir. You have to know the boundaries of the fight before you can set foot into the arena."

From the moment we met, Malachi has expected so much of me. Again and again, he's challenged me to find new ways to fight, to utilize every weapon at my disposal. "I'm tired."

"I know."

I allow myself to lean on him for five slow breaths. When I straighten, he releases me easily. I don't feel more centered, but with each path that's removed from my options, my intent becomes clearer. There really is no other way.

Back in the bedroom, I'm not even surprised to find the closet filled with a wide variety of clothing. A quick check confirms that it's in both my and Malachi's sizes. I suspect the other rooms have the same for Rylan and Wolf. "I still don't understand how you were able to outfit so many places on such short notice. Isn't it a concern that doing so will draw my father's notice since he's hunting us?"

"We used an intermediary. He's someone who isn't a known ally to any of us." Malachi motions at the room we currently occupy. "Though we didn't use him for this one."

Curiosity sinks its barbs into me. It's such a welcome distraction from the constant cycle of desire and fear and anger that it leaves me breathless for a moment. After a brief internal debate,

I pull on a pair of leggings, thick socks, and a knit sweater. "Will you tell me about the person who owns this house?"

"It's not my story to tell." He dresses as quickly as I did. I'm mildly amused to discover that his clothing options are more of the same—fitted pants and a loose white shirt. Malachi really is as eclectic as Wolf when it comes to his clothing, even if his style is more understated. Slightly. He turns toward the door. "But if you ask Rylan, he might tell you."

"I will." I follow Malachi back into the living room. One of the other men has gotten the fire going, and the cozy impression of this room only gets stronger with flames sending light dancing across the ceiling and walls.

Wolf is once again dressed in his customary trousers, suspenders, and graphic T-shirt. Rylan surprises me, though. I half expected him to have a suit on, but he's got lounge pants and a knitted sweater. His feet are bare. I stare at them for a long moment, my chest feeling strange. It's such a small thing. Bare feet. People go barefoot all the time. I don't know why the sight of *Rylan's* bare feet has my heart beating oddly against my ribs.

I drag my gaze to the fire. A much safer subject.

Wolf claps his hands and rubs them together in something like glee. "Now. Let's get down to it."

11

WHEN WOLF FINISHES DETAILING THE TERMS OF THE demon bargain, the silence is thick enough to cut through with a chain saw. Rylan is so still, I don't think he's breathing. Malachi keeps clenching and unclenching his fists.

I shift in my seat in the middle of the couch. "We didn't promise anything."

"And you won't." Rylan cuts in before Malachi can say whatever he's stewing on. "Those terms are unacceptable."

I straighten my spine. "Everyone in this room is making sacrifices to ensure I become heir so we stop being hunted. I'm willing to make sacrifices, too."

"I swear to fuck, Mina—"

Again, Rylan cuts off Malachi. "There are too many potential pitfalls. Time moves strangely in the demon realms, which is something Wolf already brought up. Beyond that, we don't know how your seraph bond might work with demons." He shakes his head. "If it tries to bond with whoever bought you at auction, they will kill you before letting themselves be bound. The cost is too high."

"We can bargain on my safety." I don't know why I'm arguing this. Ultimately, he's right. No matter what my feelings on the matter are, if all three of them are in agreement, then I need to listen to their opinions. Rushing forward because I feel guilty is foolish. "There's room for negotiation."

"It won't save you." Malachi crosses his arms over his broad chest. "The demon who kills you will face punishment, but you'll still be dead."

I open my mouth but change my mind before I tell him it's a reasonable risk. Judging from the look on his face, he won't thank me for saying as much. "If you're all in agreement..."

"We are." Malachi's words sound like a threat.

Rylan nods. "It was a far-fetched option at best. The cost is too high."

"You know how I feel, love. The only way I'd agree is if Azazel took you for himself, and he won't. He's focused on another."

I sigh and slump back against the couch. "Then I guess that option's out." Which leaves only the path we're on. Get pregnant. Become heir. Commit patricide. "What did you two find out from my father's hunters?"

"He knows." Malachi says the words so simply, it takes several beats before they sink in.

I push to my feet, earlier exhaustion forgotten. *He knows.* "What does he know?"

"That you're enough seraph to have their power and all that that entails. He suspects you bonded with at least me, if not the others, but he doesn't have a way to confirm it."

This is bad. Really, really bad. "How? How could he possibly know that much?"

"Your magic left a signature of sorts when the blood ward broke." Wolf rubs his temples. "It's not something I considered, but even if I had, it couldn't be helped. Your father isn't old enough to know what you are, but apparently my cousin decided to embrace his ambition further and handed over the information for a hefty sum."

Rylan crosses his ankle over his knee. Of all of us, he looks most normal. Which isn't to say he's relaxed; I don't think I've ever seen Rylan relaxed, even if he's wearing something casual right now. He leans back. "Ultimately, this changes nothing. If he wasn't aware of Mina's bloodline before, he would have become aware once he caught her again. The plan remains the same."

"Does this mean you're going to actually participate?" Wolf drawls. He snaps his suspenders in a steady rhythm, his eyes cold. "Or will you continue to play the martyr and whine about how you didn't want this?"

"None of us wanted this," I say.

They ignore me.

Rylan narrows his eyes. "Forgive me if I wasn't thrilled with how things played out."

"No, I don't think I will. Forgive you, that is."

I glance at Malachi, silently imploring him to step in, but he's watching the other men intensely. Surely he has some thoughts about this? I don't care if Rylan and I have fucked three times in the last three days. I'm not going to compel him to participate in this race to conception. The bond is bad enough; having a child together when he's not fully on board is a particularly nightmarish scenario.

"Don't stop there, Wolf. For once in your life, speak clearly."

Wolf pushes slowly to his feet. His eyes flash crimson. "You're a fucking coward, Rylan. You were full of plans and strategies to free Malachi from his prison, but the moment we found a way through—a way that *you* suggested and participated in—you start crying about regrets. Why are you willing to keep playing the victim and holding yourself at a distance from what you truly want? We are *right here*."

Rylan's eyes have gone pure silver. "Do tell me what I want, since you seem to know."

"Of course I know. You want what we all want." Wolf flings a hand in Malachi's direction. "But that's not the problem, is it? You've pined for Malachi since your falling-out. You were prepared to do what it took to reclaim that relationship. It's *Mina* you didn't bargain on."

"I do believe I've said that myself." For all his icy tone, Rylan looks ready to fly across the room and rip into Wolf with his bare hands.

"Poor Rylan, knocked on his ass by a pretty little seraph and her magic pussy." Wolf snarls. "It must be fucking terrible to love the chains she's unwittingly wrapped around you. That's the real problem, isn't it? It's not that you hate the bond. You fucking *love* it."

Rylan shoves to his feet, but he only gets one step before Malachi's there. The bigger man catches his shoulders. "That's enough."

I tense, expecting a confrontation. Rylan looks ready to commit murder, and from the way Wolf is leaning forward, he's willing to meet Rylan halfway. But Malachi's presence between them shifts the energy in the room. It's still dangerous. So fucking dangerous.

But there's an edge of desire now, where before there was only violence.

"Is it true?" Malachi's words are so low, they're almost lost in the crackle of the fire.

Rylan curses. "Yes."

Malachi drops his hands. "Stop punishing us for what's going on in your head."

Just like that, I can *feel* Rylan's emotions. The conflicting spiral of need and rage. A hurt that goes so deep, it makes my bones ache. Malachi all but ripped out his still-beating heart when he left Rylan. A loss he's never gotten over, one he's never *allowed* himself to get over. He's nursed that wound like the grave of someone beloved, tending to it every single day for so long it boggles my mind.

No wonder he hates me.

He arrived, ready to play knight in shining armor for the man he loves, only to find Malachi wrapped up in me. Even before Malachi gained his freedom, my presence meant Rylan had to throw away a decade's worth of plans and rush to the house to ensure he didn't lose his chance entirely.

I understand all this in the space of a second, and then the feeling is gone entirely as he gets his shields back under control. My eyes burn and I close them to try to keep the tears inside. Rylan won't thank me for the intrusion, and if he thinks I pity him, he'll hate me all the more.

I'm sorry.

Words I can't say. Not if I want this to have a chance to work. "I'm sorry."

For a second, I think I've forgotten myself and said those damning words aloud. But no, that's not my lips forming the syllables, not my deep voice speaking. I open my eyes to find Rylan staring at me. "I'm sorry," he repeats.

The bond gives a pulse that has me damn near vibrating out of my skin. I scrub at my sternum, but it does nothing to dissipate the sensation. "I understand."

He turns to Malachi, who doesn't release his shoulders. "Things change, Rylan. How I feel about you hasn't, not in all this time. But it was never going to be just the two of us for eternity. I'm not built like that."

Rylan shudders out a sigh. "I understand that now." He glances at me again. "I suppose it's not a bad thing to have an abundance of love."

Love.

Love.

He's not in love with me. He barely likes me. I can't argue something's changed in the last couple days, but it's not *love.* I would know. Wouldn't I?

Maybe that's not what he's saying. Maybe he just means it's not outside the realm of possibilities now. Or something.

He gives another of those deep exhales. "I'm done fighting it. I want everything. You. Mina." He glances at Wolf. "Even this asshole."

"Be still my heart."

Malachi is still looking at Rylan. His shield must be firmly in place, because I don't get so much of an echo of what he's feeling. His expression gives me even less. "On your knees."

Rylan doesn't hesitate. He sinks down to kneel at Malachi's feet. I stare in shock. Even on the night when we awoke my powers, Rylan was hardly submitting to anyone. It never occurred to me that he would submit to Malachi, that he would look utterly at peace while doing it.

"You know what to do."

Rylan reaches for the front of Malachi's pants with shaking hands and undoes them. It's so silent in the room, I can hear his soft exhale as he takes out the other vampire's cock. Malachi knocks his hand away and wraps a fist around himself. He guides his blunt head to Rylan's lips. "No teeth." He doesn't appear to need an answer, because he doesn't stop his forward movement, feeding his cock into Rylan's mouth.

Heat surges through me at the sight. Malachi can be merciless when he's so inclined, and how he is with Wolf—and now Rylan—feels very different from how he is with me. He's crueler, but I know Wolf loves it. Judging from the erection tenting the front of Rylan's pants, he loves it, too.

"They look good, don't they?"

I jolt. I was so busy watching Malachi fuck Rylan's mouth, I didn't even notice Wolf moving to stand behind my chair. He leans over the back of it and rubs his nose against my neck. "They have something special. Always have. Do you find that threatening? You'll never be able to touch it, seraph bond or no."

I might laugh if I could draw a full breath. Does he think he's telling me something I don't already know? I recognized the bond Malachi has with Rylan the moment the other vampire showed up. Just like I recognized the history he and Wolf share. Because of that, when I answer, I'm able to do it honestly. "No. I don't find it threatening."

"What a marvel you are." Wolf hooks the bottom of my sweater and moves back enough to tug it over my head. "We can't let them have all the fun, can we?"

"I like to watch." I bite my bottom lip as he cups my breasts. "Unless you have a better idea."

"I might." He dips a hand beneath the band of my leggings and cups my pussy. I keep my gaze on the vampires before us as Wolf slides his fingers through my folds. Malachi has his hands on either side of Rylan's head and he's thrusting forward roughly, forcing the other man to take every inch of him. Rylan has his hands on Malachi's hips, but he seems to be encouraging the violence of the moment. I catch a glimpse of claws, which only further confirms that.

They're really beautiful together.

"Malachi won't come in Rylan's mouth," Wolf murmurs, the very definition of a devil on my shoulder. He presses the heel of his hand to my clit as he pushes two fingers into me, and then three. "He's saving that seed all for you. He'll let Rylan get him close, and then he's going to come over here and fill you up." He licks the curve of my ear. "And then Rylan's going to do the same as soon as Malachi's finished with you."

I whimper. "But…"

Whatever I was going to say disappears as Malachi pulls back. He traces Rylan's lips with his cock, his eyes gone pure black. "You've denied me too fucking long, and I'm reclaiming what's mine."

"Yes," Rylan whispers.

Malachi grabs Rylan's throat and hefts him to his feet. "I'm going to come inside our little dhampir, and then I'm going to take your ass while you fuck her."

Wolf chuckles against my neck. "You should feel how her pussy clenched at that. She's on board with this plan."

I try to hold still and not lift my hips to fuck Wolf's fingers. "I can speak for myself."

Malachi finally looks at me, his hold on Rylan's throat causing the other vampire to do the same. "Well, little dhampir. Are you on board with this plan?"

"Yes." As if there's any question. I honestly wasn't sure we'd ever get to this point, where we were all in rhythm with each other. It might not hold once we're through and a new day comes, but I won't do anything to tip the balance in the wrong direction right now.

I want this too bad.

"Hold her down, Wolf."

"With pleasure." Wolf moves before I have a chance to protest—though I'm not sure what I'd protest—and grabs my wrists. He guides them up to the corners of the back of the chair.

The position leaves my chest fully exposed and gives me nowhere to hide.

I don't *want* to hide, but I can't stop the instinct that demands I fight being held down. I can't budge Wolf. The knowledge sends a forbidden thrill through me. These three vampires can do anything they want to me, and there's not a damn thing I can do to stop them. I don't *want* to stop them, a fact we're all readily aware of.

They can feel my emotions, after all. There might be a sprinkling of fear, but it only ramps my desire hotter.

Malachi pushes off his pants and stalks to me. He shoves my legs wide, looping them over the arms over the chair. There's nowhere to hide now. I can do nothing but whimper as he rips my leggings down the center seam. He doesn't even bother to push them all the way off my legs, just slides them down to my knees so he has no barriers to my skin.

He guides his cock, still wet from Rylan's mouth, into me. Even with Wolf using three fingers to ready me, my body fights the intrusion. Malachi's just too damn *big*. He plants his big hands on my thighs, pushing them up and back, holding me down as he continues his unrelenting advance.

Watching his thick length disappear into my pussy is almost enough to make me come right then and there. He's so fucking huge. His cock spreads my pussy obscenely, and I can't shake the feeling that he's stamping his ownership onto my very soul.

As if he can sense the direction of my thoughts, he growls. "You might have the bond, little dhampir, but we do, too. You're ours as much as we're yours."

12

OURS.

Gods, that's so sexy. Malachi sinks the rest of the way into me, and I whimper. "Yes." I don't even know what I'm agreeing to. Yes, I am as much theirs as they are mine. Yes, I want this to be equal. Just...yes.

Malachi fucks me like he really does own me. Like he knows my body even better than I do. He unerringly finds the spot inside me that has me going melty and hot, squirming as much as I can while so effectively pinned in place. I try to touch him, but Wolf tightens his hold on my wrists. That, too, only heightens my pleasure.

"Let go, little dhampir." Malachi grips my thighs tighter. "We have all night. This doesn't end when you come."

His rough words cut through the last of my resistance. He's right, after all. I don't have to hold out, because we're not done until *they* are. The strange buoyancy in my chest gets stronger.

Gods, *is* this love? I don't know. It's not like I've had much experience with it or even had a good example of what love looks like.

The relationship between my father and his people, his partners, isn't love. It's control and abuse. The same goes for how he treats his children, even the ones who weren't born disappointments like me.

When it comes to love, I'm feeling my way through a lightless room and hoping I don't fall into a pit of spikes. How I feel with Malachi and Wolf and Rylan is nothing like I've experienced before. Does that make it love? I don't know.

There's too much I don't know.

Malachi shifts one hand to my lower stomach, playing his thumb over my clit. He knows my body *so fucking well*. Even with my head spinning from thoughts of love, my body has no reservations about taking the pleasure he deals and embracing it wholeheartedly. I orgasm with a cry. Malachi keeps up that decadent touch until the waves recede. Only then does he pound into me, chasing his own pleasure. The fire flares hot behind him, the flames licking out of the fireplace for a moment, and then he's filling me up, grinding into me until I've taken every last drop.

He leans down and presses a surprisingly sweet kiss to my lips. I barely have a chance to sink into it before he's moving away and Rylan is taking his place. I tense a little, expecting the same rough fucking we've been getting up to lately, but he coasts his hands up my body, lingering at my hips and sides and breasts, until he lightly clasps my throat with one hand. His eyes haven't gone back to normal, still shining silver in the low light of the room. "I'm done fighting this. Are you?"

There's only one truthful answer to his question. "Yes." I'm done fighting all of it. I could spend the rest of my life railing about how unfair are the turns fate has delivered me. It's even the truth. I've been dealt a rough hand. Bemoaning that until the end of time, though? That traps me in the victim mindset.

It keeps me from appreciating the good things that have been dealt alongside the bad. No matter the events that brought us to this place, I have three bloodline vampire men at my side, all of us aligned in a single goal. I don't need an army to take my father's compound from him, not with Malachi, Wolf, and Rylan.

I catch a glimpse of Malachi coming back into the room, a bottle of lube in his hands. Oh gods, this is happening. My whole body goes tight in response. I twist a little and look up at Wolf. "And you? Are you choosing us, too?"

"I'm hurt you have to ask, love." He gives me his mad grin. "I don't turn down demon deals for just anyone."

This isn't like the night we awoke my powers. We had an agenda and pleasure was the method to deliver the endgame. That's not what tonight is about. Tonight, we're choosing each other.

Malachi closes a hand over Rylan's shoulder. "There's no going back after this."

"There was no going back the moment we chose this method of breaking the blood ward." Rylan devours me with his eyes. "I've adjusted my expectations."

With anyone else, that would be faint praise, if it was praise at all. The way he says it? It's as if he leaned down and dragged his tongue up the center of my body. He drifts his fingertips over my stomach, and I'm not surprised to find them tipped with claws yet again. There's a strange beauty to how seamlessly he shifts between human form and animal. Knowing he could kill me as easily as breathing shouldn't be sexy, but I'm far beyond worrying about what I find sexy with these three.

In my chest, the bond hums in a way I can only describe as happily. This feels so fucking right, I can barely stand it.

Malachi clasps Rylan's jaw with his other hand. "No biting Mina."

"You don't have to worry. I won't lose control again."

He hesitates. "Not tonight. Not when it's still so new. Next time."

Rylan finally nods, though he's still watching me as if he wants to consume me in slow, decadent sips.

Malachi's thumb traces over Rylan's bottom lip. "Bite me instead."

At that, Rylan's eyes go a little wide and a little hungry. "Okay."

Now it's my turn to clear my throat. "Can we, uh, move this to the floor or a couch or something? This chair restricts movement."

"That's the idea, little dhampir." Malachi runs his hand down Rylan's chest to wrap his fist around the other vampire's cock. I bite my bottom lip. Gods, that's hot.

It only gets hotter when Malachi drags Rylan's cock through my folds. Up and down. Up and down. Teasing both of us while he has total control. I try to surge up, but Wolf shifts both my wrists to one hand and coasts his other down my body to press against my stomach, pinning me further.

"Please!"

"Not yet," Malachi murmurs. "Rylan made us wait for an entire month. A few more minutes won't kill either of you."

"It might." I whimper as he circles Rylan's cock over my clit. Every muscle in Rylan's lean body appears carved from stone. He's gripping the armrests of the chair like he might rip them off, but he makes no move to stop Malachi's torment.

"It won't." Wolf pinches my nipple, making me gasp. "You should pierce these. Imagine how much fun we'd have with them. Maybe even get a little chain between the two that I could tug when you're riding my cock."

There isn't enough air in the room. I squirm, and Malachi responds by tapping Rylan's cock against my clit.

Wolf watches avidly even as he moves to my other breast and works that nipple until it's a hard peak. "Yeah, I think I'd like that a lot."

Body jewelry isn't something I've thought overmuch about, but I like the picture he paints. I like it a lot. I drag in a breath, trying to put my thoughts in order. "Wouldn't I heal too fast for them?"

"Pure silver won't let you heal completely." He bites his bottom lip, a tiny stream of blood descending from the puncture. "It would always hurt a little, for as long as you have them."

"Oh." The word comes out as a squeak.

"We'll talk about it later." Malachi notches Rylan's cock at my entrance. "Don't move." All three of us hold perfectly still as he shifts away and picks up the lube he retrieved earlier. He returns to press against Rylan's back. "I enter you, you enter her."

"Okay." Rylan's voice has gone low and gained a rumble.

His cock twitches against me, and I can't be sure, but I could swear it gets even bigger.

But Malachi doesn't move yet. He dips down and presses an openmouthed kiss to Rylan's throat. The arms of the chair creak as Rylan fights to hold still, to submit. His silver eyes are practically creating their own light source now. They only get brighter when Malachi bites him. It's not a gentle one. With me, he's usually careful not to tear the skin any more than necessary, to keep the damage to a minimum.

He's not being careful with Rylan.

The wound is ragged and large, and blood spurts onto my mostly naked body for several seconds before Rylan's healing takes over and the flow slows. Malachi drags his tongue through the blood on Rylan's neck. "Now."

His hands disappear behind Rylan, and I don't need to see details to know he's spreading lube over his length and the other vampire's ass. Rylan moans a little and pushes the head of his cock into me. Knowing that he's mirroring the advance of Malachi's cock into his ass...

"Fuck," I whisper.

"That's the idea, love."

Another inch. Another mixed moan from the three of us. For his part, Wolf seems content to draw patterns in the blood spatter on my chest and stomach, but that won't last. He's not one to sit idly by when there's pleasure on the table.

The sound of wood breaking and then the arms supporting my legs are gone, torn apart by Rylan's attempt to maintain control. Wolf lets loose his wild laugh. "In that case..." Another splintering sound and suddenly the back of the chair is gone, too. He catches me before I fall, using his body to support me. "Hand me the lube, Malachi."

For a moment, I think Malachi might argue, but he hands the bottle over. It takes a little adjustment to get the broken remains of the chair out of the way and move to the spot before the fireplace, but we end up in nearly the same position. Wolf wastes no time working his cock into my ass from below me while Rylan and Malachi kneel between my spread legs. Even though the men like to come in my pussy, Wolf loves to fuck my ass. We've done it more than enough times that I'm making impatient sounds as he slides deeper.

More, more, more. I need more.

Once he's seated his full length inside me, he kisses my neck. Malachi guides Rylan's cock back to my pussy.

He was big before. Even without his bloodline power coming into play, Rylan is large. Having Wolf's cock in my ass as Rylan works into my pussy? He's almost too big. He has to fight for every inch, and his low moans tell me Malachi is doing the same into his ass. Eventually, a small eternity later, he's seated fully within me.

I can't catch my breath. The first initial push was a pleasant warmth, but now I feel like my skin is going to burn right off my body. The sensation only gets stronger when Malachi starts to move. We're all sealed so tightly together that as he braces a hand on Rylan's shoulder and starts to fuck him in slow, deep thrusts, the other three of us rock together with each stroke. I'm pinned between Rylan and Wolf's bigger bodies, spread wide open by their cocks inside me, and none of us can do anything but take what Malachi gives.

The bond flares inside me. Except it's not a flare, not really. What happened that first night together was a flare, overwhelming and near-violent. This feels more like a flower unfurling. "More," I gasp.

Malachi gives us more. He plants his fists on either side of our hips and starts fucking Rylan's ass. Starts fucking all three of us. That's what it feels like. I can't quite explain it, and pleasure makes it even harder to process what I'm feeling, but...

I can feel *everything.*

Malachi's fierce possessiveness, his determination to claim all of us as his in a way that can't be broken.

Rylan's relief, the way this moment feels like all the broken pieces have clicked together in his chest, turning into something whole.

Wolf's joy at finding what feels like home, his anticipation over the chaos and bloodshed to come.

I can feel all of it.

I cling to Rylan—or maybe it's Malachi—as I shatter into a million pieces. This isn't like any orgasm I've had before. It goes on and on, pleasure so acute, it's agony. I can't stop coming, am barely aware of the men losing control in and around me. Something hot and wet hits my neck. Wolf, biting Rylan. Hot pinpricks sear my hips. Rylan's claws. A roar fills the room that sounds like the noise a forest fire makes as it rampages. Malachi.

Higher and higher, more and more. I can do nothing but ride the wave, a piece of flotsam tossed about by a hurricane. There is freedom in submission, and I find it in this moment. My last shred of strength dissipates. I go limp, a marionette with its strings cut.

Someone curses, and everything goes black.

13

I WAKE UP IN A PILE OF BODIES AND COVERED IN blood. For one heart-stopping moment, I think I've killed them, but Malachi groans and shifts, and then Wolf makes a sound that might be his mad laugh if every one of his vocal chords had been shredded beyond repair. Rylan's half on top of me, and I can feel him breathing.

Alive.

I exhale slowly. I feel like I've been hit by a truck, and then they backed over me a few times for good measure. Everything hurts. Not just muscles and bone but down to a cellular level. My throat feels like someone took sandpaper to it while I wasn't paying attention. It takes me three tries to speak. "What the hell was that?"

"Fucking seraph bonds," Rylan murmurs against my throat.

I can't tell if he's angry or just exhausted. "Apparently there's more to this bag of tricks than I realized."

I blink at the ceiling, waiting for his words to make sense. They don't. "Please explain," I manage.

"Later."

As much as I want to argue, he's right. I don't have the strength to form more than a few words at a time. They start to shift, and every one of them is moving like they feel as terrible as I do. What *was* that?

Rylan rolls off me, and I try to sit up. I get as far as planting my hands on the floor and the sight that greets me has me staring blankly. Surely those aren't my hands? Except they can't be Rylan's because I can see *his* hands where he lies next to me. "Um."

"Um?" This from Wolf. He's thrown his arm over his eyes as if even the light of the fireplace is too bright for him.

I flex my hands. They move. Which means they're mine after all. I swallow hard. "I have claws."

"Cute."

I flex them again. Each of my fingers is tipped with a shining silver claw. They're almost pretty, dainty and deadly with a wicked curve that's designed for slicing and tearing. "No, I mean I literally have claws. Like Rylan."

"Funny story…" Wolf lifts his arm off his eyes and flicks his fingers. Sparks dance in the air above him, morphing into a ribbon of flames. It dissipates almost immediately, but there's no denying that it was there.

That puts the strength back into my body. "What the hell is going on?"

Rylan's arm shifts to some kind of large cat and then back to human. "I still have my powers." He frowns. "But I can feel the flames, too. And the blood coursing through all three of your bodies."

Now that he mentions it, I can as well. The fire sounds almost like a siren song. It makes me want to reach out and...

The flames flare up in response.

I silence the thought and they die back down to normal levels in response. "This is bad."

"Is it?" Malachi hefts himself up to lean against the couch. He looks as exhausted as I feel, but there's a contemplative expression on his face that means he's thinking six moves ahead. "This will be incredibly useful."

"If Cornelius gets ahold of us, it will be useful to *him*." Rylan doesn't sound as icy as normal. He's too busy toying with the flames of the fireplace, making them surge and flow. "This is fascinating. It feels so different from mine."

I start to wrap my arms around myself but stop when I scratch my skin with my new claws. "How do I put them away?"

"Concentrate." Rylan's still distracted with the flames. "Picture it and they'll retreat."

How am I supposed to concentrate when my world has just been turned upside down *again*? Having seraph powers is one thing—I still haven't come to terms with it. Having bloodline powers? My throat gets tight and panic flutters in my chest. "I don't know how to control this."

"Mina—"

"I don't have training. I can't shield. I have no experience."

My voice is getting higher and higher with each word, but I can't make myself stop. "This is too much! I'm going to get us killed."

"*Mina*." Malachi crawls to me and pulls me into his arms. "It will be okay. This is a good thing."

"It doesn't feel like a good thing. It feels like I'm a fucking freak. How am I supposed to deal with this?" I wave my hand, and it's as if my powers snag on every drop of blood in Wolf's body. He jerks several inches to the side. "Oh my gods." I clench my fists and bury my face in Malachi's chest. "I'm sorry. I didn't mean to."

Wolf laughs, the sound a little hoarse. "Kinky."

"It might not be permanent," Malachi says slowly. "Relax. Let's get cleaned up and we'll figure it out like we have everything else up to this point."

"By fighting and snarling at each other?"

His chest moves against my cheek in a soundless laugh. "*Together*."

The chair is ruined and blood has stained the rug. There's no cleaning this up. I dread what replacing those things will cost, but the men don't seem overly worried about it. When I ask, Rylan gets a strange smile on his face. "The owner of this place has cleaned up worse messes than this. It will be fine."

With *that* cryptic statement, we all head into the master bedroom and take turns showering off. Under other circumstances, it might have turned into some sexy fun, but I'm barely managing to stay on my feet, and the men don't seem like they're doing much better. Malachi orders us into the massive bed before we fall down, and no one argues with his command. That, more than anything, speaks to how fucked up things are right now.

I end up wrapped in a blanket, cuddled between Wolf and Rylan while Malachi reclines on Rylan's other side. It's a strange sort of puppy pile, but it feels effortless. Especially when Rylan idly sifts his hand through my hair.

As tempting as it is to close my eyes and let them comfort me with their presence, we have to talk about this and we need to do it now. I twist a little to see Rylan's face, but not enough to dislodge his hand in my hair. "Did you know this might happen?"

"No." He closes his eyes, his expression strangely peaceful. "But the seraphim weren't exactly sharing the inner workings of their powers with everyone else. The bond was common knowledge at the time, and everyone was aware that it could cause compulsive obedience, but beyond that, it wasn't clear." He frowns a little. "Though it doesn't make sense that it would share powers like this. Plenty of vampires who were forcibly bonded would rather die than stay linked like that. I can't imagine they'd hesitate to use more power against the seraph who held their leash."

Killing the seraph likely meant killing every vampire they were bonded to. "Is that possible even with the compulsion?"

"Yes."

He doesn't need to elaborate. If he says it's possible, then it is. Sharing power the way we have would make it much easier to kill the seraph involved. "Maybe it happened because we chose this. Tonight, I mean. Maybe the bond responded to that willingness."

"That seems likely." Malachi's staring at something off in the middle distance. "In the end, it doesn't change the end goal or the plan. We'll stay here as long as we can. It will give us time to figure out if this is temporary and teach you what you need to know to control them."

That makes me laugh, but not like anything is funny. "It takes bloodline vampires decades to learn to control their powers."

"Who told you that?"

I start to snap back but realize that he's right. My father was my source of all my vampire lore until I met Malachi. It stands to reason that he would keep information close to his chest, even from his children who *did* inherit his magic. Information is just another kind of power, and my father never parts with power willingly. "Well, shit."

"Cornelius really is an asshole." Wolf chuckles. "A month should be more than enough time. Maybe less since you have all three of us helping. You'll be fine, love." He says it with such confidence, I almost believe him.

On the other hand, when has *anything* come easily for me?

"In the meantime, we maintain the course." Malachi looks down at me. Even as tired as he obviously is, there's heat in his dark eyes. An answering pulse goes through me. No matter what else is true, I love having sex with these men. *Love* it.

I...love them.

I won't say it. Not now. Maybe not ever. It's too new and raw and unknown. No matter what we've chosen for the future, the power between us is so precariously balanced. Telling them what I feel is asking for trouble.

Coward.

I ignore the little voice inside me and close my eyes. "Yes. We'll maintain the course."

I don't remember going to sleep, but I wake up with Rylan's mouth on my breasts and Wolf's tongue in my pussy. It feels like a fever dream to glance down and find Malachi's mouth wrapped around Rylan's cock. A fever dream, but so right my heart gives a painful thump in response. This is how it should be. The four of us. Together. This is how it *is* now.

Wolf moves back a little and flips me onto my side. Rylan and Malachi move to adjust, Rylan shifting down to tongue my clit and Malachi moving with him. And then Wolf is pressing into me. "Love your ass," he murmurs against the back of my neck. "Can't neglect this pretty pussy, though."

Rylan chuckles against my clit, and I shiver. "This…"

"Shh, love." Wolf clasps my jaw and urges me back so he can claim my mouth even as he thrusts deeper. "Just a dream."

I reach down and sift my fingers through Rylan's short hair. He's rubbing my clit with his tongue slowly, teasing my pleasure higher. This entire experience feels lazy in the best way. No one is rushing. We're simply giving and receiving pleasure. Each orgasm they deal me feels like a little death that builds on the last one, a slowly rising tide.

At least for a little while.

Nothing good lasts forever. Not even vampire sex.

Eventually Wolf's strokes lose their smooth rhythm and he bites my neck as he pumps me full of his come, setting off a chain reaction of another orgasm from me. I cry out, pinned between his cock and Rylan's mouth. It's too good. I can't take any more.

I don't have a choice.

Malachi eases off Rylan's cock and licks his slit, but his eyes are on me. "Fill her up, Rylan. I want all three of us mixed inside that perfect pussy."

Rylan nods, his eyes nearly glowing. He barely waits for Wolf to pull out of me before he's yanking me down his body and shoving his cock into me. We're still moving slow, still maintaining that lazy vibe, but it feels different with Rylan. It always seems to feel different with Rylan, like he's barely restraining himself from shredding the bedding and driving into me until he tattoos his essence on every inch of my body.

Once again, pleasure rises in a wave. I recognize the feel of Wolf's power sending my blood to pulse in my clit and nipples. I shiver around Rylan's cock, clinging to him as I get swept away yet again. How much pleasure can one body hold? It feels limitless in this moment.

He buries his face in my neck as he comes. I feel the tiniest nick of teeth, but a swipe of his rough tongue and all evidence of it is gone.

Or if would be if we weren't in bed with two other vampires.

Malachi grips the back of Rylan's neck and pulls him off me, his expression forbidding. "No teeth."

"She's recovered." He seems to arch up into Malachi's touch. "Besides, Wolf bit her."

"That's different."

"I'm recovered," I confirm. I'm more than recovered. Now that I'm fully awake, the lingering exhaustion from last night is gone. I feel...really, really good. Like I could run a marathon and then go climb a mountain, and maybe finish off the day with some deep sea diving. I touch my knee. The scar my father gave me is gone, just like the pain and limited mobility are gone.

In fact...

I sit up and look at my body. *All* my scars are gone. How did I not notice it before? I registered that they were fading faster than was humanly possible, but there were still many lingering. At least there were until last night.

I don't like it. Those scars were linked with my memories of surviving. I went through *so* much, and nothing my father and his cronies did could break me. They hurt me, scarred me, damaged my body, but they couldn't break me.

Now, all those scars are only in my head. It feels strange.

I twist to look at Malachi. A sound almost like relief whispers from my lips at the sight of his scarred chest. That, at least, hasn't changed. I want him to tell me the story someday. Would he still do it if the scar disappeared? The thought isn't logical, but I can't shake it. "Come here."

He kisses me, a slow, drugging claiming. I sink into the feel of him, let myself be buoyed by his steadiness. This. This is all that matters. I can face down all the wild magic in the world as long as Malachi remains steady at my side.

He flips me over onto my hands and knees. It gives me a great view of where Rylan and Wolf lean on each other against the headboard. They're not exactly cuddling, but they're not *not* cuddling, either. They watch us with a barely sated hunger.

With vampire blood, there's little to no recovery time. If I didn't have to stop to eat, we could fuck for days, weeks, months. Maybe even years.

Malachi nudges my legs wider and then he's guiding his cock into me. A slow, steady intrusion that has my breath gasping from my lungs. Every time. *Every time.* It always feels like the first time with him, like he's claiming me all over again. "You can take more," he murmurs.

More of his cock?

More orgasms?

I don't get a chance to ask. He braces one hand on my hip and one on my shoulder and picks up his rhythm. At this angle, every stroke slides his cock along my G-spot. I whimper, and my mind goes blank. I'm vaguely aware of my fingertips tingling as they morph into claws, of me shredding the bedding just like I'm sure Rylan wanted to do. He might have restraint. I have none. I can feel my blood surging through my body, a new awareness that no doubt comes from Wolf's bloodline. Part of me screams to control these foreign powers, but I can't think straight with Malachi fucking me like this.

I close my eyes as yet another orgasm bears down on me. I'm so focused on my pleasure, I almost miss the scent of smoke.

Then I'm coming, and I know nothing at all.

14

"YOU HAVE *GOT* TO STOP FUCKING ME UNTIL I PASS out." I watch the smoke waft from the remains of the little fire I apparently set when I orgasmed.

Wolf smothered it with a pillow and now he's trailing his fingers through the smoke with a grin on his face. "Remember when you gave Malachi grief for doing this very thing?"

I groan. "In my defense, he burned a ring around us and nearly collapsed the entire floor. You three might survive a little bit of being burned alive, but I won't."

"You will." Rylan trails a finger over my claws. "I may be wrong, but after last night, I'd wager not much can kill you."

Easy for him to say. I try to frown, but the expression won't stick. I'm too content. "You literally almost killed me...four days ago?" Was it four days? Five? I'm not sure anymore. We hardly kept a regular schedule in the first place, but all the running has messed up my internal clock. Being in a house carved into the interior of a mountain isn't helping, either.

"That was four days ago." He pricks his thumb on my claw and lifts it to press to my lips.

The blood zings through me. My mouth tingles, and I have to work to restrain myself from trying to bite him. My teeth aren't like a vampire's. I'll just gnaw on him without some help from a blade.

Or my claws.

Rylan grins as if he can read my thoughts. "Go ahead."

I waste no time scrambling up to straddle his stomach. After the smallest consideration, I lightly drag my pointer finger down the center of his throat, leaving a trail of blood in its wake. Delight courses through me. I don't need the men to cut themselves for me any longer. I can do it myself. I grin and lean down to drag my tongue up his throat.

"Don't get him riled up again, little dhampir." Malachi lies next to us on his back, his head propped on his arm. "We need to leave the bed and do some training."

"I don't want to train," I murmur against Rylan's skin. It's not quite the truth; I know training is vital, both the combat and now magic. But it's hard to remember that with Rylan's hand on the back of my neck, lightly massaging me as I drink from him in little sips.

"Up, Mina."

I groan a little, but I obey. It's only when I'm standing that I get a good look at the bed. "We are going to owe the owner of this house so much money."

"It's fine." Malachi rises and disappears into the closet. He comes back into the bedroom a moment later dressed in a pair of gym shorts and carrying workout clothing for me—leggings, a bra, and a tank top.

I pull the clothing on but pause when Rylan and Wolf make no move to do the same. "Aren't you two coming?"

Wolf drops onto the bed and rolls until he's pressed against Rylan's side. "Oh, someone will be *coming*." He reaches down and closes his hand around Rylan's cock.

"Insatiable," Malachi mutters.

Rylan clears his throat. "We'll join you in a little bit."

Malachi leads the way out of the bedroom, and I can't stop the goofy grin from pulling at the edges of my mouth. I'm not naive enough to think that everyone's worked through their baggage. That's not how anyone functions: humans, vampires, or seraphim. Especially when they have the sheer amount of history my men share. Their issues will crop up again and again as time goes on.

But after last night and this morning, I finally believe we can navigate our way through whatever happens.

We end up in a fancy gym that has everything from free weights to various machines to a nice mat for sparring. I whistle softly. "Wow."

"It's a nice change of pace." Malachi rolls his shoulders. "First, sparring."

This time, I don't bother to complain. He's right that I need this training, and Malachi is an excellent teacher. Even if I want to toss him out a window from time to time because he's so damn unrelenting. This morning is no different.

An hour later, I'm dripping sweat and every muscle in my body is trembling from exertion. Malachi executes a flawless move that has me spinning through the air and landing on my back hard enough to drive the breath from my body. He twists around to look down at me. "You should have seen that coming."

"I did." I wheeze. "Reflexes too slow."

"Get faster."

"Trying."

He reaches down, and I take the offered hand, letting him pull me to my feet. He gives me a slow smile. "You're getting better."

"Don't say 'I told you so.'" I can't quite pull off the grumpy act. My goofy grin keeps peeking through. I press my fingers to my cheeks. "This is ridiculous. I can't stop smiling."

"You look happy."

Happy. The concept is as foreign as love is to me. But if I can feel one, surely it's possible to feel the other? I let my hands drop. "I think I am happy?"

"Are you asking me or telling me?"

"I don't know." I laugh. "I have no business being happy. We still have so much to accomplish. We're nowhere near safe. We—"

"Mina." The quiet command in his voice cuts me off. Malachi takes my face in his big hands. "Life is challenging enough without putting qualifiers on happiness. It passes, just like fear and anger and horror pass. Enjoy the feeling while we have it."

I make a face. "That's not exactly comforting."

"I wasn't trying to be comforting." He leans down and presses a light kiss to my lips. "Now, on to the magic."

Strangely, the magic training is more difficult than the sparring. Malachi sets me up as if we're going to meditate, but his low voice talks me through the process. It feels like trying to bench-press a car. I can *feel* the magic, but it's so overwhelming, I can barely envision wrapping my hands around it, let alone guiding it to my will.

I don't know how much time passes before he calls it quits, but it feels like I've learned nothing at all. "I don't care what you all say. This is going to take years."

"You can already feel the movement of your powers. That's the hardest part."

I give him the look that statement deserves. "If that's the hardest part, I should be able to do more."

"It's the first day, little dhampir. Have some grace for yourself." He holds the door open. "Let's feed you."

"Shower first." I pull the wet fabric of my tank top away from my skin and cringe.

"Shower first," he confirms.

It takes twice as long as it should because we get distracted with each other's bodies, and by the time we make it out, both Rylan and Wolf have disappeared. I eye the bed. "How many rooms does this place have?"

"More than enough." Malachi wraps an arm around my waist, guiding me to the door. "But if we want to reduce the amount of damage we do, we should confine fucking to this room."

Because we're destined to lose control and continue to trash whatever room we're in. I press my hand to my mouth, as if that's enough to hide the grin. "That sounds like a good idea."

"Mmm." He tucks me against his body as we head for the kitchen. "You *are* happy."

He would know. If the lesson earlier is anything to go by, I won't be successfully shielding for some time. "I suppose I am."

"It looks good on you."

We find the other two in the kitchen, Rylan making a pot of coffee and Wolf staring at the fully stocked fridge as if it might jump out and bite him. "Humans and their desire for options. It's food. Why should it need to be so fancy?"

"Spoken like a vampire."

He motions at the fridge. "Pick your poison."

"I'm more than capable of making my own food." I slip out from beneath Malachi's arm and walk to the fridge. As ridiculous as I think Wolf's being, he's right; there are a truly overwhelming number of options here. I grab an apple and wander to the pantry door a few feet away. Thankfully, the owner has a veritable storefront of power bars. I pick a couple and head back into the kitchen.

All three vampires look at me with disbelief.

Rylan raises his brows. "All those options and you choose *that?*"

"I don't know how to cook all that many things and I'm starving, so I don't want to take the time to deal with it right now. Power bars were good enough for me before. I don't see why they shouldn't be good enough for me now."

Malachi's frowning as if solving a complicated problem. "I thought you preferred them because they're easy to carry on the run."

"That is one of the reasons I prefer them, yes." From their expressions, they're not going to let it go, so I feel compelled to explain. "While there are humans and dhampirs in my father's compound, they're hardly a priority compared to the vampires. The food they're provided is designed to keep them alive and healthy so they can continue to act as walking blood banks and, at times, breeders. Power bars were the tastiest of the bunch."

Wolf shakes his head slowly. "That is rather pathetic, love."

"It is what it is." I take my power bars and apple to the counter wrapping around half of the kitchen island and sit down. "Good food matters less than keeping myself alive. That's always been the priority."

"It can still be the priority if you're eating other food." Malachi crosses his arms over his chest.

Rylan pours coffee into a mug and passes it to me. "I'll learn to cook." When all three of us stare at him, he shrugs. "It's a necessary skill if we have someone who consumes food."

"Rylan—" I don't know what I'm going to say, because I never get a chance to finish that sentence.

There's a burst of power in the room and all the shadows seem to surge forth to a center point. One moment, there's the four of us. The next, Azazel stands in our midst. He slides his hands into his pockets and gives the room a long look. "Interesting."

As one, the vampires explode into motion. Malachi grabs me and shoves me between him and the wall, his big body blocking out the rest of the room. I hear Rylan curse and a scuffle. Peering around Malachi's arm finds Wolf pinning Rylan to the counter.

He gives the other vampire a shake. "Focus. He's a demon. If you attack him, he'll slice you to pieces."

Azazel examines his fingertips. Are they sharper than they appeared at first glance? I can't tell from this angle. The shadows move around him almost as if alive. For a moment, I get the impression of a hulking beast with giant horns curving from its head. In the next breath, it's gone, and there's only the handsome dark-haired man who seems to carry an aura of danger on a level I've never experienced before meeting him. Even having been in the same room as he was two days ago isn't enough to make me used to the sensation.

The demon shifts, and the three vampires tense in response. His slow grin says he did it on purpose. "What a charming little nest you've created, seraph. Have you considered my deal?"

"She's not making any deal."

Azazel cuts a look at Malachi. "I didn't ask you." He narrows dark eyes. "Fire-bringer. I'd like to see how you do in *my* realm, vampire. We demons can show you what true fire means."

"Now, now, Azazel." Wolf lets loose his high, mad laugh. "There's no need to prove you're the baddest motherfucker in this room. We're all convinced." Rylan opens his mouth, but Wolf slams his hand over it before the other vampire can speak. "Answer the nice demon, love."

Right. Okay. I take in a slow breath. "I've decided not to make a deal with you." There's only the slightest tremor in my voice to indicate how stressful this situation is.

"Pity." Azazel examines his fingertips again. This time, I'm *certain* they're sharper than they were. They haven't shifted the way Rylan's—and now mine—do. The fingers are exactly the same. Just...sharper. "Ah well. Since we're such good friends, Wolf, I suppose I should tell you that there's a group of six vampires heading up the mountain in this direction. Good luck." He disappears as suddenly as he arrived.

For one breathless moment, we're all perfectly still.

As if on cue, there's a niggling feeling at the very edge of my mind. I didn't notice it with Azazel's presence masking everything, but now there's no denying the fact. It's identical to what I felt last time. I swallow past my suddenly dry throat. "He's right. They're here."

Then Malachi surges forward. "Wolf, with me. Rylan, protect Mina."

"Of course." He sweeps me off my feet before I can take a single step. The house passes in a rush, Rylan sprinting down a hall I haven't had a chance to explore. He ducks into a room filled with monitors and slams the door shut.

I watch him pull down a heavy steel beam to drop into the crossbar over it. "That seems excessive."

"If I were your father, I would send a team from the front and a second, smaller, team from the back." Rylan drops into the chairs in front of the monitors and starts clicking buttons.

I concentrate, but I can only feel the irritation in one direction. "*Is* there a back to this place?"

"Of course." He frowns at the monitors and keeps clicking, flicking through the pictures so fast it makes me dizzy. "Only a fool wouldn't leave a back door to escape from."

Of course. How silly of me not to realize that was the case. "Who *is* this person?"

Rylan's fingers pause over the keyboard. "He was a…friend."

"Was?"

"He died some time ago. His granddaughter owns this house now, and she's responsible for most of the upgrades. For reasons I'm not prepared to get into, she was willing to offer it as a place to stay."

I have more questions, but they'll have to wait. Rylan's stopped on two screens. One depicts the road we drove in on. A single vehicle works its way up. It almost looks like a tank, armored plating beefing up the sides and roof and small windows not offering much in the way of weak points. I've seen that vehicle before. My father owns three of them. He uses one every time he has to leave the compound.

Surely he didn't come here himself?

"It's not him." Rylan shakes his head. "As I said, it's a good decoy, but this is the true strike team." He motions to the second monitor.

It depicts a trio of masked individuals. It's so dark, it takes me far too long to understand what I'm seeing. No trees. No rocks. No dirt. A hallway very similar to the ones we've been traveling since arriving yesterday.

"They're inside."

15

I LEAN CLOSE TO THE MONITOR. "WHY CAN'T I FEEL this group?"

"They must be masking their presence." He doesn't look happy at the revelation.

I could argue that maybe my lack of expertise is to blame, but there's no time to figure out the why. All that matters is that they're in the house and we're outnumbered. "What do we do?"

Rylan clicks a few more buttons. "You're not going to do anything. They're barely inside. It will take them time to get here." He stands and rolls his shoulders. "I'll get to them before that happens."

I'm moving before I register my own intent, shifting to stand between him and the door. "Not alone."

"Mina." He smiles slowly. "No matter what else is true, here

I am the apex predator. Once I'm out the door, hit this button."
He motions to one in the sea of them. "It will shut off the lights."

"Vampires have superior eyesight in the dark."

"They still need some light to be able to see. They won't get
it in here."

Because there are so few windows. I drag in a breath, fear like
a live thing inside me. "That means you need light to see, too."

"Yes, but sight isn't the only way to get around. Smell is just
as useful." He closes the distance between us and kisses me hard.
"Bar the door behind me. If the worst were to happen, there's
a hatch below the desk that will take you out. It's narrow and
uncomfortable, but you'll be free."

If the worst were to happen.

That would mean that Rylan is incapacitated. I drag in a
breath. "If you think that's a possibility, don't go."

"Mina." Gods, the way he says my name. Tenderly, as if testing
it out in the space between us. "No matter what else is true, we are
warriors. We can only run and hide for so long." He brushes his lips
to my forehead. "I care for you. I won't let them take you." Rylan
lifts me easily out of the way and sets the bar across the door aside
before I have a chance to react. Then he's gone, sliding out into the
shadows of the hallway. His body ripples as he changes, shifting
into a monstrous wolf that looks like something out of a nightmare.

I shut the door and wrestle the bar back over the door. It's
heavy enough that I don't know if a human woman could manage
it. If I wasn't terrified out of my mind, I would wonder again
what kind of woman this granddaughter of Rylan's friend is, but
I have bigger things to worry about.

I hold my breath as I push the button Rylan indicated. Instantly, all the cameras go dark. Did I fuck something up? Even as the worry takes hold, the cameras flick back to life, their images taking on a green tint that indicates night vision.

The giant wolf that is Rylan appears and disappears in flashes, running full out down the warren of hallways. He barely pauses at the doors. I can't be certain, but I think he shifts one hand to open them each time. It makes me dizzy trying to track him, so I turn to the intruders instead. They're all dressed in black and wearing masks that hide everything but their eyes, which now glow eerily in the night vision. They could be anyone.

I don't know the layout of this place well enough to figure out where they are, and it's not as if Rylan left a convenient map to track their progress against. All I know is that he's moving quickly, and they don't seem to have been slowed down much by the lack of light.

On the other set of screens, the vehicle is stopped. I catch blurs of movement that might be a fight, but my eyes can't track it to tell for sure. No matter what advantages seraphim might supposedly hold over vampires, their physicality isn't one of them. They're faster and stronger. I can feel Malachi and Wolf through the bond, but all I'm getting is a direction and approximate distance. It doesn't make it easier to tell what's going on.

Trying to follow the action will just give me a headache. I keep one eye on that screen but turn the rest of my focus to the intruders actually in the house. They've gone still. I examine the buttons before me, finally finding one that seems to allow audio. A horrifying howl echoes through the speakers.

Rylan's caught their scent.

I peer at the screen, but they don't seem nearly as terrified as I would be in their position. Being hunted in the dark by a monster, unable to see the threat coming at them.

The staticky sound of a radio. A tinny voice I can barely pick up. "We're in position."

The small hairs at the back of my neck rise as the tallest person in the group lifts the radio and says in a horrifyingly familiar voice, "Round them up."

Father.

Oh gods, Rylan's in over his head. No matter how easily he can cut through normal vampires, all my father has to do is get a word out and he'll flip the tables entirely. He can order Rylan to hold still and cut him into little pieces and there's not a single thing I can do to stop it.

I scan the buttons, looking for some kind of intercom, but it's too late.

On the screen showing the outside, the vehicle explodes. I stop short, staring in horror as vampires emerge from both sides of the road. There's a flurry of blurred movement, a flash of fire, and then everything goes still.

Two bodies fall to the ground, and even in the dark I recognize Wolf and Malachi before the other vampires close in, piling onto them to trap them. "No," I whisper.

"*Stop. Be still.*" My father's voice brings me back to the other screen. He pulls the mask from his face. "Flashlight."

One of the other vampires provides a flashlight and he clicks it on. Right before them, less than ten feet away, is Rylan. His body is low to the ground—obviously my father stopped him right before he pounced—and he quivers as he fights the command.

"Pretty thing," my father murmurs. "You'll make an excellent rug in my great hall."

"No!" They can't hear me. There's no way any of them can hear me.

My father flicks his fingers. "*Sleep.*" He watches with interest as Rylan slumps to the ground. "Bind him with silver." As his people rush to obey, he turns and finds the camera overhead. "Are you watching from some bolt-hole like the rat you are, Mina? All the suffering to come could have been avoided if you'd done the one task I set out for you." He shakes his head. "This is on your head. Now, be a good girl and wait for me. I'll be along shortly."

Something wet and hot slides down my cheeks. I press my fingertips there, strangely surprised to find that I'm crying. All this time and effort, and he's outplayed me once again. If I open the door and turn myself in, he might—

What am I saying?

He won't let any of the men go. Three bloodline vampires in one fell swoop? It's a feather in my father's cap like no other. He won't stop with a blood ward this time. No, he'll want to ensure any progeny of this trio of bloodlines stays within his control. He'll do whatever it takes to make it happen, including drugging and torturing my men.

A sob bursts from my throat and then I'm moving, shoving the chair back and fumbling down at the floor beneath the desk for the hatch Rylan said was there. I can't help them if I'm taken, too. I'm not sure I can help them if I'm *not* taken, but I have to try to fight. They've sacrificed too much for me to do anything else.

I find the hatch and wrestle it open. I can hear my father's voice, vibrating with power, but it doesn't work well long distance. His will presses on me, demanding I hold still and obey, but it's dampened from being conveyed through electronics. Because of that, I'm able to slip into the dark square beneath the desk and pull the hatch closed behind me.

Rylan was right; it's a tight fit. I descend the ladder in perfect darkness, the walls so close, they almost brush my shoulders.

I couldn't feel the weight of the mountain while in the house, but here it's almost overwhelming. Even without seeing my breath, I know it's ghosting the air in front of me. A shiver works its way through my body, and I pick up my pace. There's no telling how long I have before they find the security room, how many minutes it will take them to break down the door and give chase.

Endless minutes later, the ladder ends and my feet find solid ground. I reach around, trying to get a feel for where I am now. My foot nudges something. A box. Inside, I find the familiar shape of a flashlight. I hold my breath, praying to gods I'm not sure I believe in that the batteries are still full.

The light clicks on.

I exhale slowly and take a look at my surroundings. It appears to be a natural cave of some sort, the walls close and slanting. There's only one path forward, so I have to hope that it leads to the exit. Spending years wandering this place, lost, while my men are tortured and bred against their will is out of the question.

The box that held the flashlight also has a thick coat that's only slightly too large, a pair of boots that are also slightly too large, and a pack of bottled water. It's not quite a bug-out bag, but it's close enough. I pull on the boots and coat, instantly feeling better now that I'm not freezing. I glance up into the darkness where the hatch is, but there's no sound or movement. Down here, I'm completely cut off.

Except I'm not really.

I can still feel the men through the bond. Rylan somewhere above and to the right, Wolf and Malachi to the left.

If my father transports them, the bond will react poorly.

Shit.

I pick up my pace, hurrying through the cave in the only direction I can walk. Maybe under other circumstances, I'd marvel at the cold beauty of this place or consider how it makes me feel like I've left our world behind entirely.

It takes less time than I would have guessed for me to see a sliver of light ahead. I click off the flashlight and move forward slowly, all too aware that this might be yet another trap. If my father was able to find the other entrances, surely he could find this one?

Except when I step out into the sunlight and turn back to look at the cave entrance, it's nearly invisible. And I'm standing six inches from it. Someone would have to truly know it was here to find it.

Still…

I consider my options. I know where my father will take my men. He rarely ventures out of his compound to begin with, and it's more than equipped to keep captives. It's hardly the first time he's tried something of the sort.

I suppose I'll have to try to keep pace with them as best I can to avoid the bond lashing at all of us. I'm not sure what will happen if they're taken too far from me, but I don't want them to suffer while we find out.

A branch cracks somewhere off to my left. I react on instinct, crouching down next to a bush and holding my breath.

"I can see you, you know. That's a god-awful hiding spot."

A feminine voice. It's not familiar, but I hardly know all my father's people by voice alone. "If you come closer, I'll kill you."

"Cute, but I don't think so." A woman steps into view. I blink like a fool in response. She's a tall white woman with a mass of wavy brown hair and an athletic build, clothed in what looks like military gear designed to camouflage the wearer. The gun slung over her shoulder isn't her only weapon. I count at least three knifes that I can see, one long enough that it might be termed a sword.

She's also human.

She eyes me. "You're Rylan's seraph."

Surprise flares. I wouldn't have thought he'd tell anyone about my identity or what that might mean between the two of us. "Who are you to him?"

"A friend. Sort of." She lifts her gaze to the mountain behind me. "I take it things went poorly. The alarms have been blaring since those assholes breached my security. Where is he?"

"They took him." I can feel him moving, but there's a sluggish nature to the bond that makes me suspect they drugged him.

I don't know what drug can incapacitate a vampire, but of course my father is aware of it and has it on hand. "They took all of them."

"Well, fuck."

"That about sums it up." I twist, trying to estimate the growing distance. We have miles and miles to play with, but I'm on foot and they'll be in a car before too long. "I have to go."

She narrows inky eyes at me. "I don't suppose you have a plan."

Not even close. "Of course. I'm not going to let him harm them."

The woman sighs. "I guess I'm at your disposal, at least for transport and the like. Though I'm not storming any castles for you, princess."

I can't afford to trust her, but at the same time, I can't afford to reject any help out of hand. "Why would you help me?"

"My family owes Rylan a debt we can never repay." She doesn't say it like she's happy about it. "Since I'm the matriarch of the family now, that means it's on me to keep balancing the scales."

I eye her. I'm hardly an expert on humans, but she doesn't look much older than me. "Who *are* you?"

"Oh. That." She adjusts the position of the gun across her back and offers her hand. "Grace Jaeger. I'm a monster hunter."

I shake her hand, feeling numb. "Wouldn't you consider me one of the monsters?"

"Definitely." She says it so easily. "But like I said, the whole debt to Rylan thing means you're safe enough with me."

I'm out of options. I run my hand through my hair. "We have to follow them. Do you have a vehicle?"

"Come on."

Her vehicle, if it can be termed such, is an off-roading beast with two seats and yet more weapons. Grace climbs behind the wheel. "Which way?"

I point north. "They'll be heading for Montana where my father's compound is."

"I see." She worries her bottom lip, a small line appearing between her dark brows. "We can't drive this the whole way, but there's a good stopping point a few hours from here that will take us in that general direction."

It will have to do. "That works."

She guns the engine and then we're off, flying over a trail that barely seems to exist. The engine is too loud for easy conversation, which is just as well. I don't know this woman, and all I can focus on is the worry about what comes next.

My father *took* my men.

I close my eyes and welcome the anger that knowledge brings. Better that he'd taken me instead. At least I know how to survive in that compound, though that was back when he actively underestimated me. I doubt he'll make the same mistake again.

Nausea rolls over me in a wave, and I have to open my eyes. What the hell? I press my hand to my chest and try to focus on the area in front of the vehicle, but it doesn't help. Another wave, stronger this time. "Pull over."

Grace glances at me. "What?"

"Pull over!"

She slams the vehicle to a stop, and I barely get out of it in time to lose the power bars and apple I ate earlier. I keep dry heaving for several long moments as my stomach tries to exit my body.

I have never thrown up once in my life. I don't get sick at all, not really. I search the bond as best I can, but it doesn't seem to be originating from there. What the hell?

Another wave of nausea nearly has me dry heaving again.

"You okay?" Grace gives a rough laugh. "You're not, like, pregnant or something, are you?"

Surely not.

Except...

I close my eyes, feeling with my power on instinct alone. I've gotten really good at feeling the parameters of the bond. Searching within my actual body isn't all that different. To be thorough, I scan myself from head to toe. There, nestled in my lower stomach, I find it.

The tiniest, most fragile spark of life inside me.

I open my eyes. "Holy shit."

I struggle to my feet to find Grace offering me a pack of mint gum. "Don't get back in here until you chew through one of these. I'm super sensitive to smell and puke breath is gross."

"Thanks," I say faintly, my mind still spinning.

"Is there a reason you're muttering 'holy shit' at the forest after you throw up?" She sounds vaguely curious, almost like she's asking out of politeness.

If I'm really pregnant, it means I have what I need to fight my father. It would be significantly simpler if I also had my men at my side, but I'll make do. All I need to do is get onto the compound and make a public declaration. It will take careful planning. I can't think about it right now.

I press my hand to my stomach, and the little flicker of life seems to flare brighter in response. I wish I could be happy. This is what we wanted after all. Except my being alone and stranded with some strange *monster hunter* while my men are taken captive by my father was never part of the plan.

"Turns out you were right." I swallow hard. "I'm pregnant."

KEEP READING FOR A LOOK AT *QUEEN* BY KATEE ROBERT

1

I NEVER GAVE MUCH THOUGHT TO PREGNANCY. NOT even when my father sent me to Malachi's home with the intention of sacrificing me, body and blood, to the trapped vampire. At the time, I'd planned on escaping or dying before he knocked me up.

Look at me now.

I slump back against the tub in the cheap motel bathroom. My head spins and sweat slicks my skin. My mouth tastes... Well, best not to think about that too hard or I'll start retching again. I drag myself up to the sink and brush my teeth for the tenth time today. An exercise in futility. I'll be puking again before too long.

As if being sick isn't bad enough, my thoughts feel as fuzzy as the inside of my mouth. I need to be planning, to come up with some idea to free my men, but I barely have the energy to move.

My father has Malachi, Wolf, and Rylan, and I should be coming up with a way to rescue them.

Instead, it's all I can do to navigate the crappy hotel room where I currently reside.

I stagger out of the bathroom to find Grace lounging on one of the two queen mattresses in the hotel room, flipping through channels with a bored expression on her face. I still don't know enough about this woman, for all that she's helped me. She's a white woman with long dark hair and an athletic build. She also seems to want to be anywhere but helping me. Yet she hasn't ditched me. Her pile of weapons is carefully arranged on the desk, and once again I'm left wondering about this one-woman army.

She glances at me and raises her brows. "You're a mess."

"I know." I drop onto the free bed and wait for my stomach to decide if it's going to rebel again. After a harrowing moment, it settles and I exhale in relief. "Did you have a chance to look over the plans of the compound I drew up?"

"Yeah." She sits up. "They're nicely detailed. You have a really good eye for security and what to look for."

Of course I do. I'd been planning on escaping the first chance I got. I had my father's patrols, security measures, and everything mapped down to the smallest detail, and I'd had to do it by memory because if I wrote something down and he found it... I shudder. "At least growing up in that hellhole was good for something. We can help the men." We *have* to help them.

"About that." Grace won't quite meet my eyes. "I'm going to be brutally honest with you—"

"When are you anything less than brutally honest?" We've

only been traveling together for two days, but Grace's bluntness is both a balm and an aggravation. She doesn't lie; she doesn't even bother to cushion harsh truths. I sit up. I'm about to get another of those harsh truths right now. "What's wrong?"

"It's a lost cause, Mina." She doesn't look happy about it. "If I had a trained team, we *might* be able to get in and get out, but the odds already aren't good because of what we're dealing with. By your own estimate, there are hundreds of vampires in that compound. Even if they were only turned and had no powers to speak of, those numbers just aren't surmountable. It doesn't matter that only a third or so of them are trained soldiers. Any vampire is a threat to the success of a rescue effort. Add in the fact that all your father has to do is speak and we lose, and it's impossible."

"No." I shake my head. This isn't right. None of this is *right*. Malachi and I were just talking about plans a few days ago. We should be safe in the mountain stronghold that is owned by Grace's family. We should be prepared to win.

Instead, I'm alone with a woman who obviously doesn't want to help but just as obviously feels obligated to try. And my men? They're currently enjoying the questionable hospitality that comes with being my father's captives. I shake my head again, harder this time. "I refuse to believe that."

"They'll kill us." She doesn't say it unkindly, and somehow that makes it worse. "If you're lucky, they'll kill you, too. If you're not, your father will lock you up somewhere until you birth that little monster and *then* he'll kill you."

I press my hand to my lower stomach where the little spark

of life pulses in time with my heart. "It's not a monster. It's barely a cluster of cells at this point."

Grace opens her mouth but hesitates. When I stare, she finally says, "It's making you weak. You can barely use your powers, and you're sleeping more than you're awake right now."

I drag my hand through my hair. She's right. I haven't been operating at anything resembling normal capacity since I found out I was pregnant a few days ago. I will admit to not knowing much about pregnancy, but it seems like the symptoms have come on far too quickly. I should have *weeks* before I start to see side effects.

Unless you've been pregnant longer than you or the men realized.

I clear my throat. "I know. It's not ideal, but—"

"There are options." She still won't meet my gaze. "You don't have to keep it."

I freeze. My brain knows what she's saying, but it still takes me a few moments to let the offer sink in. Terminate the pregnancy. I press my hand to my stomach. Hard not to be resentful of the little presence that isn't quite a presence. I thought pregnancy was my option to take my father's throne, but I can't even get in there, and I certainly don't have the energy to fight. If I show up and publicly declare myself his heir...

I want to believe it will stick.

I desperately need it to be true.

But there's a chance—and it's even a large chance at this point—that he'll do exactly what Grace says and lock me up until I have the baby and then kill me for all the trouble I've caused. More, my half siblings are hardly going to support my claim. As far as they're concerned, I'm a powerless dud, which means I'm not a legitimate contender for the head of clan.

If I had an army at my back, it wouldn't be a question. I could bust open the front gates, make my claim in front of the entire compound, and take over. No one could stop me. No one would *dare* stop me.

But with just me and Grace? And me being incapacitated more often than I'm not?

She's right to bring up this option, no matter how conflicted I am talking about it. "It's not just my decision," I finally say.

"Actually, it is." She shrugs when I look at her. "Hey, I'm not telling you what to do. I'm just presenting options. Ultimately, it doesn't really matter which way you land on the topic, because it's not going to change the end result. We have no way into the compound that doesn't get us both dead."

I wish she wasn't right. I press the heels of my hands to my eyes, trying to *think*. "There has to be a way." I have no allies. I wouldn't even know where to start looking for them, and it would take far too much time. Grace seems to be a lone wolf. Who the hell could we possibly call for... I drop my hands. "Azazel."

"*What?*"

The familiarity in Grace's tone nearly distracts me, but I'm too focused on what appears to be the only option we have. He asked for seven years of service to break the seraph bond I have with my men. We might not have agreed to those terms, but if he can do *that*, surely he can offer some kind of real help to get my men back. Even if it's the same price, seven years is *nothing* compared to potentially hundreds of years under my father's control.

I might not live that long, but Malachi, Rylan, and Wolf certainly will. It means there's no release waiting in the wings. Just endless suffering. I can't let that happen. I *won't.*

"*Mina!*"

I blink. "What?"

Grace is on her feet and looks like she can't decide whether to shake me or leave the room entirely. She rocks back on her heels. "Say that name again."

"Azazel." This time, I'm paying attention. I see the way she flinches and narrow my eyes. "How do you know that name? Do you know him?"

"No." A sharp shake of her head. "But I know *of* him. I know what he does." The way she speaks, it sounds like she's talking about more than just deals. Like there's an element of sinisterness to it I don't understand. Having met Azazel, I can't say he's anything less than terrifying, but he was rather frank about the terms. There were no hidden catches or trickery. It's more than I can say for how my father operates.

"He seemed fair," I say finally. "Or, if not fair, then honest." He spelled out the terms clearly. Maybe the contract itself would have been a problem, but we didn't get that far. The men drew the line at my paying seven years of service.

"Shows what you know." Grace paces back and forth in the small space at the end of the bed. She pulls her ponytail out and starts braiding her hair in short, agitated movements. "Are you aware of what he does? He rips women away from their families and most of the time they never return."

The way she talks, it sounds like she's speaking from personal experience. I frown. "Who do you know that's bargained with him? And seriously, he only bargains with women? That's kind of…outdated, isn't it?"

"Take it up with the demon." Grace drags her fingers through her long dark hair, disrupting her braid and restarting it. She's long since changed out of the camouflage hunting gear in favor of faded jeans and a plain white T-shirt. Somehow, it doesn't make her less intimidating…or less dangerous. She drops her arms and pins me with a look. "He took my mother."

"You mean your mother made a deal." I don't know why I'm arguing this. I don't owe Azazel anything. Wolf made it extremely clear how dangerous the demon is. If anything, I shouldn't be listening to Grace since she has just as much experience with demon deals as I do at this juncture. I wrap my arms around myself. "What were her terms?"

She turns away. "I don't know. The last time I saw her was the night he came to collect. I know she made a deal, but I've never been able to get more information. I…" She exhales slowly. "I don't know how to summon him. Do you?"

Do I?

I know what Wolf did. It seemed simple enough, at least in theory. His bloodline vampire power is the ability to manipulate blood itself. Thanks to my seraph half, I've somehow managed to acquire that ability, along with Rylan's shape-shifting and Malachi's fire. It *would* be enough…except I got these powers less than a week ago and I've had exactly one training session with Malachi to learn how to control them. Since then, I've barely had the energy to keep up with Grace, let alone try again.

I close my eyes and try to walk back through what Wolf did to summon Azazel. A blood circle that became a blood ward of sorts. I think. He fucked Malachi in it, but I don't know if that's part of the ward or just because Wolf is, well, *Wolf*.

As far as I can tell, after creating the ward, he did nothing at all. Azazel showed up quickly after Malachi and Rylan left, but Wolf didn't even say his name before the shadows went weird and the demon appeared. It has to be the circle. Which is a problem because I don't know the first thing about creating a blood ward. "Do you know how to create a blood ward?"

"Mina, I'm *human*."

Right. Of course. I shake my head slowly. "Then no. I don't think I can summon him." Then again, maybe I'm overcomplicating things? I lift my voice. "Azazel? Can you hear me?"

"Holy fuck." Grace flings herself back against the wall, her dark eyes wide as she searches the room. The seconds tick into a full minute, and we both breathe a sigh of something akin to relief when nothing and no one materializes. Grace glares. "I can*not* believe you just did that."

I can't believe I just did that, either. I shrug, trying to pretend I'm not as shaken as I am. "It was worth a shot."

"It was worth a shot," she repeats, shaking her head. "You are out of your damn mind, Mina." Grace scoops up her backpack from the floor and a small gun from the desk to tuck into her waistband. She pauses with her hand on the door. "Get some sleep. I'm going to see about taking a look at this compound myself. I think it's a long shot, but maybe there's something you missed or something that's changed since you were there that can provide us a way in."

It's not safe for her to go scouting on her own. My father is sure to have sentries farther afield than just the compound walls, and Grace might be human and therefore not seen as a threat, but she's a beautiful human. I wouldn't put it past them to try to snatch her off the street to either be turned or tossed into my father's pool of humans who serve as mistresses and blood banks. "Grace—"

She's gone before I can get my warning out.

I mean to follow. I truly do. But one minute I'm trying to get the energy to stand and move to the door, and the next a wave of dizziness hits me hard enough that I have to throw out a hand to brace myself on the bed so I don't topple. "What the fuck?"

Is this an attack?

I try to push my magic out, to sense, but it's like I'm wrapped in a thick cotton straitjacket. I can't feel anything at all. With a curse, I turn inward. A quick body scan leaves me even dizzier. *Oh no. This is so bad.* I let my hand drop, feeling ill in a way that has nothing to do with morning sickness. I'm not being attacked, at least not from the outside.

It's the baby.

It's draining my magic.

ABOUT THE AUTHOR

Katee Robert is a *New York Times* and *USA Today* bestselling author of contemporary romance and romantic suspense. *Entertainment Weekly* calls her writing "unspeakably hot." Her books have sold over a million copies. She lives in the Pacific Northwest with her husband, children, a cat who thinks he's a dog, and two Great Danes who think they're lap dogs. You can visit her at kateerobert.com or on Twitter @katee_robert.